Glimmer in the Dark

Glimmer in the Dark

COZY DUBOIS

Book Cover Art and Design by Otte (Ottelote).

Interior Formatting by Cozy DuBois.

Editing by Mikko Lahna.

Paperback ISBN: 978-1-964386-09-6

E-book ISBN: 978-1-964386-08-9

No generative Artificial Intelligence was used in the process of developing, writing, or designing this publication.

First edition 2025

For the lonely souls and cynics who love a little whimsy.

Content Awareness

While this book includes a happy ending for the queer characters, it contains some heavier themes and explicit content. Please proceed with caution if any of the following may be uncomfortable for you:

- Explicit sexual content between two consenting adults while drinking alcohol. Includes oral and manual stimulation, and use of a vibrator. Includes detailed descriptions of male anatomy, including that of a trans man (using language such as dick and hole).

- Transphobia, acephobia, sexism, and anti-Asian prejudice in the workplace.

- References to past parental and familial abandonment.

Friday

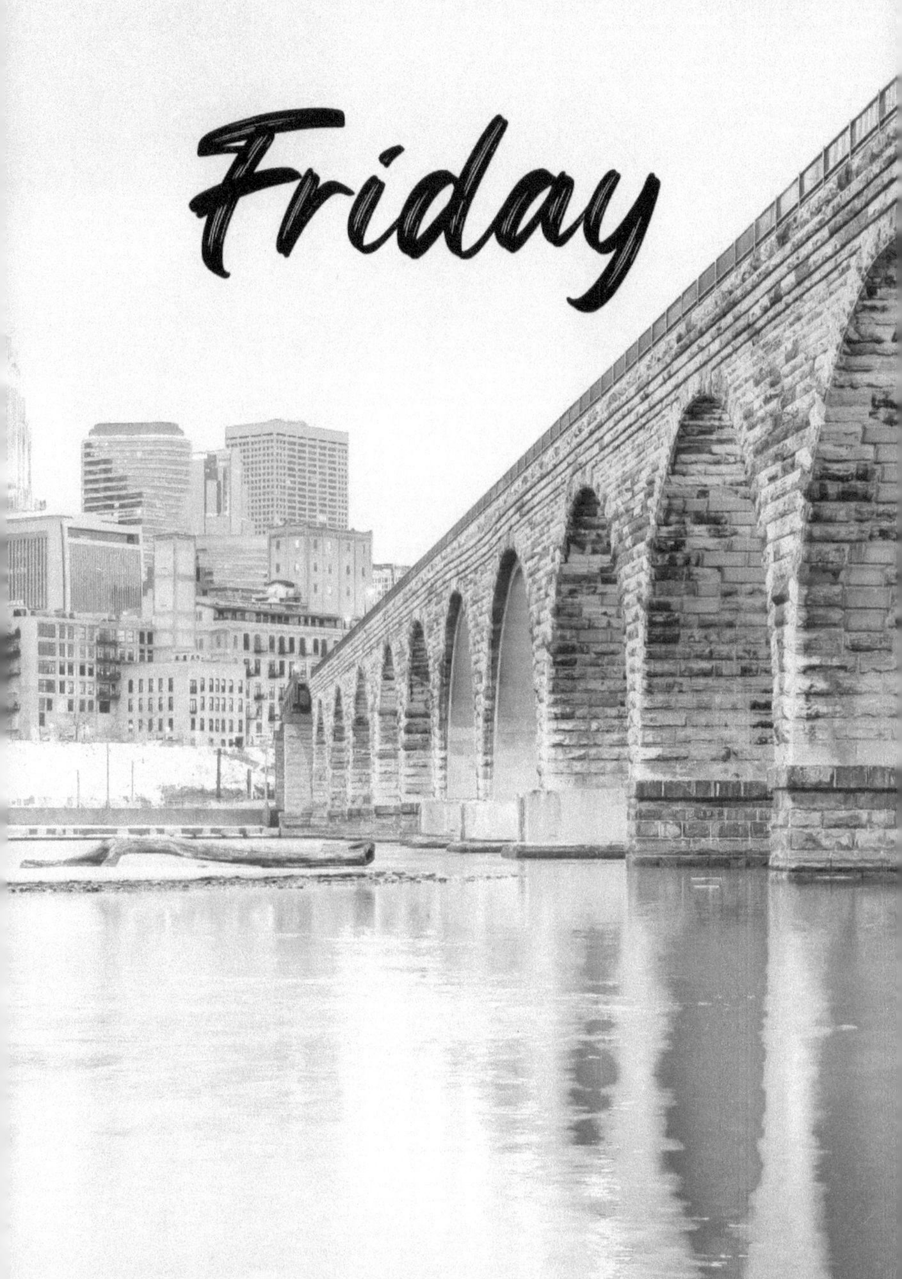

Chapter One

THE ONLY GOOD THING about this horrible, no-good, shitty-ass day is that the breakroom is blissfully empty, with the lone exception of my work wife. From her seat by the window, Gina greets me with a wave of her celery and a grim smile. I toss my lunch box with a *thunk* onto the melamine table as I collapse into the closest chair. "Gina, I would never dare speak ill of anyone at this company," I suck my teeth, glancing around to make sure we're truly alone before I add, "but Bill and Sanzhar can go fuck themselves!"

Gina has the gall to laugh.

"I don't know why you're laughing, I am dead serious!" I shake my head, my skin burning with barely-suppressed rage. That joke of a meeting has left me deflated, exhausted, and oh, so completely done with this place. I never thought Bill would stab me in the back like that, at least not in front of the whole engineering team! "Today is the day I quit, mark my words!"

"You know, Rory, you always say that," Gina says, balancing her hummus on her baby bump as she scoops some onto her celery. Her feet are propped up on the plastic chair next to me, shoes off. I'd tease her about the smell, but honestly, Gina's swollen feet would be preferable to the reheated fish and cheese currently permeating the small room. Some heinous individual must have reheated tuna casserole in the microwave. Gina takes another bite, the crunch crisp and satisfying. "We both know you are way too nice to ever mean it."

With an agitated huff, I look longingly out the window. The meeting ended an hour ago, and I'm still shaking. I wish I could go for a walk to cool my head, take a breath and watch the falls from the Stone Arch Bridge. But the winters here are too brutal for my Appalachian sensibilities. Fortunately, even the smallest glimpse of the Mississippi is enough to quiet the storm raging through me. The dark water peeks through the bare trees along the riverbank, a sliver of nature between the stone-clad office buildings and shiny glass condos in the Mill District of Minneapolis, where I live and work.

A massive river in a big city is a far cry from the crick in the holler of my childhood home, but nature is nature, and it always helps. I'll take a walk when it gets above freezing. In five or six months. Because it's only December, and even though it's been snowing since October, everyone here insists it's not really winter yet.

I've lived here long enough to know they're full of shit. It's winter.

They need to invent a city that's trans friendly, warm, and affordable. Where egotistical, blowhard bosses are not allowed.

"Well, if I don't quit, then I reckon today's the day I finally throw a hissy fit," I huff, tapping my can of sparkling water, knowing I would never. The tab opens with a satisfying crack that has me wishing for something stronger. While I may be splitting at the seams and hopping mad, I can't get fired for drinking at work. I need this job. "More'n likely, I'll say something sassy to *Sanzhar*," I sneer the name, "and he'll snitch to Bill, who'll write me up. Ooh! Maybe he'll fire me, so I can get unemployment!"

Gina snickers, which is not very validating when my skin is burning hot from how pissed off I am. "Rory, stop making me laugh. My bladder can't handle it!"

"Hush your mouth, G, it's not supposed to be funny! I'm real tore up about this!" Her giggle is so infectious, I find myself smiling along with her, despite the resentment simmering under my skin. Maybe I should stop cracking jokes if I want her to take me seriously, but that's how we always are. I chuck the lid off my Tupperware harder than necessary into my lunch box. The bright scent of cumin, cilantro and lime in the bean salad I've brought for lunch is completely and utterly obliterated by the horrific smell of cheesy tuna.

"Sorry, sorry! You're just so sweet and easygoing all the time, and with that Southern accent, you're so cute when you're angry!" Gina covers her mouth and clears her throat. Unconvincingly, as her hummus is shaking on her bump. "What happened? Tell your work wifey all about it," she says, imitating my drawl. My accent is softer than when I first moved here a few years ago, but she still teases me for it. Kindly, of course. We're the only two queer people in the office; good-natured shit-talking is to be expected. I've grown to hate this company, but I adore Gina.

When I first met her, she was incredibly rude to everyone, except me. As the admin in a start-up of all men, Gina is usually a stone-cold bitch, to keep the flirting to a minimum. She's like Dolly Parton in *Nine to Five* (happily married, and fully aware that the men in our office are creeps) meets Megan Fox in *Jennifer's Body* (gay, short-tempered, and smoking hot). Even at eight months pregnant, she's not exactly successful at convincing all these older, socially awkward guys that she's off-limits.

At first, her warmth made me uncomfortably dysphoric. However, I've come to realize that she's nice to me because

I treat her like a person, not because we're "girlfriends." Our friendship is akin to a lavender work-marriage: my presence helps keep her from getting hit on, and she's someone I trust enough to confide in. About work stuff anyway; while she probably wouldn't be too judgmental, I don't want to risk the rest of the office finding out about my personal life.

"It really don't matter, but..." We're still alone, but I lower my voice anyway. Everyone else finished lunch long ago, but I had to send out minutes for the meeting I'd barely paid attention to, on account of the swallowed rage pounding in my ears. It took me a good fifteen minutes of crying in the single-stall bathroom, and then another fifteen fighting off more waterworks at my desk, before I could even type. I'd hoped testosterone would make the tears dry up, but I'm still a big ol' crybaby. The only difference after three years is now, I can keep from bawling until I'm alone. "Bill gave the Aurora Labs project to Sanzhar."

"He didn't!" Gina gasps, the way a good friend should. Even though as Bill's admin, she must've been fully aware of the decision. "That deal is huge! That guy just started! And frankly, project management is *not* his forte."

I nod along with her. However, Bill is aware of those things too, and he *still* chose Sanzhar. "I'm just sick and tired of being overlooked. Three years, I've worked my ass off, and I'm more competent than any of these guys, smarter too—"

"Don't forget humble," Gina teases.

"I mean, shit, the way I reckon..." I gesture around the empty room as if to prove my point, because I *am* more humble. The problem with being an aerospace engineer is that all of us have enough ambition, and large enough egos, to dream of working for NASA (myself included). But not every aerospace engineer *can* work for NASA. Some of us end up in academia, or the military. And some of us wind up at start-ups, developing software for commercial satellites. But that rocket scientist ego still lingers.

Add a blowhard boss to the mix, and my ass has been fighting an uphill battle for credibility since I moved across the country for this job three years ago. It didn't help that I was a bubbly, Southern blonde at the interview. Then on my first day, I informed Bill I was transitioning. While he didn't fire me, I knew I'd have to pay my dues to get ahead.

So I have worn all the hats without complaint, stayed late and worked weekends to fix defects and test patches, taken minutes for every meeting the way everyone else assumes I will because I'm the only AFAB person in the room. My project plans have transformed productivity for the whole team. Only I can translate the indecipherable tech speak between our client's dev teams for our product managers. My ingrained Southern charm, combined with my propensity for ten-dollar words, has saved countless tense conversations and strategic relationships.

I am invaluable here, and everyone knows it.

Only for Bill to give a huge, complex, high-profile project (a deal *I* sourced) to his new protégé: some space case he poached from another software company in town. Sure, Sanzhar is brilliantly smart—I'm not so enraged to admit that his technical knowledge exceeds anyone else here, myself included—but pretty is as pretty does. He's got his head in the clouds, that one. Whenever I ask him a question he hasn't considered, he loses focus of the conversation, going deep in thought for hours, unable to switch gears to another topic until he's solved it. Brilliant, analytical, intelligent (and yes, handsome), but worth a hill of beans in a crisis.

Why on earth did Bill give my deal to *him*? At least Sanzhar had the chagrin to avoid looking me in the eye the rest of the meeting (not that he ever does), but he still didn't object when Bill announced it. He seemed to know it was coming.

My stomach churns, blood boiling all over again. I pick at my bean salad, nausea making me dread the first bite. "I should quit."

Gina tuts, packing up her lunch. “You can’t quit. This place would fall apart without you.” She wrinkles her nose at the broccoli she thinks she should eat and never does. Putting the cover on, she winks at me. “Or if you do, take me with you.”

I snort. “I guess I can wait until you’re back from leave, G.”

“Plus six weeks, so I don’t have to pay back my premium!” Gina reminds me, getting to her feet with a wince. She busies herself with starting a fresh pot of coffee. Bill is a creature of routine and ego; he’ll take it personally if his afternoon pick-me-up isn’t freshly made.

“I’ll tell you what, six months, we’ll be somewhere better,” I smile. We have this conversation all the time, counting down to the day we might blow this Popsicle stand together. Neither of us has updated our resumes in years.

“In the meantime, maybe take a vacation for once, Rory. You’ve earned it!” She ruffles my hair. The ends fall into my eyes, the faded blue dye making my mousy hair even duller. “You’ve saved up enough PTO and comp days that you can probably take my whole leave with me if you want. My wife will be so jealous, she only gets four weeks.”

We laugh together. I brush my hair back, while she picks up her lunch box and oversized water jug.

“Oh, you left something.” I hold out a brochure that was underneath her lunch box.

It’s an advertisement for a winter solstice retreat at some resort called the Starlight Lodge. The northern lights streak green across the sky on the pamphlet, above a snowy field with a geodesic dome in a pine grove. My breath catches in my throat. I love Minneapolis, but it’s been three years, and I have yet to see the northern lights. Call it naivete or ignorance, but I thought it’d be a common occurrence here.

“Oh, no, that was here!” Gina waves, already halfway out the door. “Enjoy your lunch!”

I flip it open, elbows propped on either side of the bean salad I still don’t trust myself to eat. Inside are pictures of the dome, a cozy and sun-filled bedroom, happy guests soaking in a hot spring or skiing. Most of the pictures are of the glorious aurora borealis, a sight I've been yearning for since I was the dorky kid obsessed with space. I spent my leisure time reading endless nonfiction tomes, learning how the magnetic field and axial tilt protected Earth and life from the cold violence outside of our atmosphere. My older sister and younger brother had more socially acceptable hobbies, but my parents always said they were proud of my gumption for pursuing my unconventional interests so unapologetically.

They probably regret encouraging me now.

Maybe I should take a vacation. Gina's right; I've earned one. I've barely taken a day off in years, worked enough overtime and weekends to have a heap of comp days stockpiled. I take a sip of my water. Is this worth getting my hopes up? The solstice is this weekend, but maybe this place will still have openings. I could rent a car, drive however many miles it is, to wherever this is in my new state, my new home. The snow hasn't stuck around yet, at least in the Cities, so the roads should be clear.

If the weather holds, I might could extend my stay through Christmas, to help ignore the inevitable ache that comes from knowing my family back in North Carolina is celebrating together. Without me there to "confuse" my sister's kids, or to stress my brother out by "starting trouble." Just like they've done the past two years.

I flip to the back; the resort is just outside of Fairbanks. And with that, the whole plan comes crashing down.

"Never mind," I mutter to myself, ignoring the pang of disappointment. My whole day—whole life really—has been disappointing; not going on vacation is positively minor in comparison. Flying to Alaska is already a pipe dream, let alone getting there in time for the winter solstice on Monday, a mere three days from now.

I toss the brochure on the table, just as Bill's voice booms from the hallway, followed by the quiet murmur I've come to recognize as Sanzhar's. They're headed this way. With a grimace, I finally take my first bite of bean salad, and mentally prepare to make nice with my boss and his new pet.

Chapter Two

Because I am nothing if not professional, I smile as Bill and Sanzhar walk in. Bill's in his usual too-tight navy polo, neck bulging around the buttoned collar, and pleated khakis. Between his lack of style and thinning brown hair (not that I'm one to talk, thanks to testosterone), he looks much older than his mid-forties.

Bill does not smile back, which makes me beam even harder. I probably look unhinged. While I may be estranged from my family now, my mother's insistence on good manners is still deeply ingrained. Like me, this smile can persevere through any hardship.

Sanzhar's eyes catch mine, but his smile is more of a wince. He quickly busies himself with the collar under his forest green sweater, fussing with the bow tie. Between the geek chic clothes and neatly trimmed mustache, he always looks like a nerd, but he's pretty enough to be a hot nerd. I might low-key resent

Sanzhar and all he represents (before he started, I could tell myself that everyone disliked me because I was the new one, instead of prejudice), but the man knows how to dress. Unlike me, who always looks chronically online in graphic T-shirts and hoodies, with barely any facial hair to speak of (though I am very proud of the whiskers on my upper lip; one day, they'll connect).

While not quite as tall as Bill or I, Sanzhar has a stocky build, proportionate with his shorter stature. Add in his long hair that's always in a bun, trendy glasses, and fun accessories, Sanzhar is always gussied up enough to look chic.

But he stole my project, so Sanzhar can suck a dick, bow tie and all.

Kill 'em with kindness, my mother would say. *Be so gosh darn sweet, they can't help but love you.* I swallow my pride, and greet them both, "Hi Bill! Heya Sanzhar!"

Glancing over long enough for me to know that motherfucker heard me, Bill's gaze goes cold as he turns his back, like I'm not in the small room at all. "Ah crap, coffee's not done yet." He gestures impatiently at the carafe, slowly filling with the coffee Gina started a few minutes ago. "What's a guy gotta do to have coffee ready around here? I swear, I don't know what Gina does all day. I pay her enough that I shouldn't have to wait for this shit."

Sanzhar merely offers me a quick smile and polite nod, which I barely register over the pity behind his brown eyes.

Shock and hurt slowly turn to sheer rage. My hands are shaking so hard, my bean salad falls off of my fork. Make nice with this trifling fool and his pet? I bite back the sardonic laugh, pretending to read the Starlight Lodge brochure. I stab my bean salad in an attempt to act unbothered, even though I'm so pissed off that I'm sweating up a storm. How can I make nice, when Bill is outright pretending I'm not even here? Talking shit about my work wife for making coffee for his entitled ass? First he gives the Aurora Labs project to this dweeb, and now he's ignoring my existence?

Oh, bless his heart.

"Smells delicious in here, doesn't it?" Bill booms, leaning on the counter to wait, keeping me carefully out of view. "It's my wife's specialty, Swiss cheese and tuna hot dish!"

Bill is the one who reheated nasty cheesy tuna in the microwave? Blood roars in my ears. The brochure crumples in my hand, the geodesic dome creasing around itself as my fist tightens.

"What are your plans for the holiday, Sanny?" Bill asks.

I bite my cheek to keep from scoffing. Somewhere deep down, it must bother Sanzhar that Bill calls him that. He's only ever introduced himself as Sanzhar, yet the older folks in the office follow Bill's lead. Gina and I have considered starting a betting pool about when he might finally snap (more likely, politely correct someone), but we both agree he probably never will. Sanzhar has never reacted, always smiling along politely with that aloof attitude.

Just like he is now. A barely-there polite smile on his face as he answers, "Oh, this and that. My mother—"

"Family is what matters most, this time of year!" Bill proclaims, tapping the coffee machine impatiently. Sanzhar's smile doesn't waver. "Glad to hear you're spending time with your parents. We've got party after party lined up every weekend this month, and the whole week between Christmas Eve and New Year's! I'll be so tired of my in-laws by the end of this! With the kids home from college for winter break too, I might end my vacation early to get out of the house," he laughs, as if the idea of spending time with his family is worthy of derision.

Sanzhar's smile tightens, ever so slightly, but he says nothing. Instead, his eyes meet mine. I glance back to the brochure, pretending to be fascinated by this Starlight Lodge, before he thinks I'm a weirdo for watching them when apparently, I'm not worth acknowledging.

My gut churns as I force myself to eat my bean salad. The flavor is lackluster, like I can tell the corn came from the freezer, the tomatoes from a can, in a way that it didn't when I made it last night. Even fresh, sun-warmed veggies in the peak of summer would probably taste like ash right now.

Finally, the coffee pot beeps, and Bill pours himself a cup, still rambling on and on and on to Sanzhar about all of his many plans with his parents, and his wife's parents, and his extended family reunion on New Year's Day.

My chest aches more and more the longer this jackass keeps on. The last time I went home for Christmas, I warned my family in advance that I was transitioning. Gave them a heads up that I would look different, and that they should call me Rory. They must not have realized I was serious, until I showed up at my childhood home with scraggly facial hair and a flat chest.

I'd been nervous, but excited for them to meet the real me, the happiest version of me. Only to catch a red-eye back to Minneapolis the same night, with no chance to freshen up, no invite to come in and sit a spell, not even a hug. Instead of the confused but warm greeting I'd expected—because my parents always said that only God came before family, a value I'd always shared even though I've never really believed in God—Mama burst into tears. My older sister snapped at her daughters to go play downstairs, then started praying the second the basement door closed. Like I was a demon out of Hell, instead of her sibling. Dad quietly told me it would be best if I left. At least my younger brother wasn't there yet; he would have made the real scene.

This year, like last year, I saved up enough to buy everyone presents. For the airfare back to Charlotte, and the car rental for the hour drive to the small town in the foothills of the Appalachians where I'd grown up. Just in case it all came out in the wash, like I'd assumed it would. In case they changed their minds and invited me back. In case they missed me.

But there's only a week before Christmas, and I haven't heard a peep from them in two years.

As soon as Sanzhar and Bill make their exit, coffees in hand, my eyes well up. Through my tears, the aurora on the brochure almost looks real.

"Fuck it." Fuck Bill, fuck Sanzhar, and everyone here but Gina. Fuck the god-awful smell of hot tuna and stinky Swiss! Fuck my family.

I have PTO. I have money.

And I've always wanted to see the northern lights.

Saturday

Chapter Three

"You gotta be fucking kidding me!" Elbows firmly planted on the reception desk, I bury my face in my hands, twisting the roots of my hair in an attempt to center myself. The scratched and worn patina of the wood plank I'm leaning on has coffee cup rings staining it. Somehow, that tiny imperfection is my last straw. I squeeze my eyes shut, trying to ignore my bone-deep exhaustion and frustration as it threatens to spill over and add to the damage. "What do you mean, 'no record of my reservation'?"

"No need for language, Mr. Callahan," the receptionist of the Starlight Lodge chides politely, with a slight twang I can't place. She's a tall Black woman, who looks to be around my age, with a no-nonsense frown and a frankly intimidating buzz cut. That barely-there accent hints that she is not from Alaska. "I can tell you've had a long day, but I'm trying my best to help you. Crude language is not going to make this any easier for either of us."

"My apologies, ma'am," I mutter, guilt hitting even harder than it normally would. As someone well practiced in talking people down, I can recognize when someone is using their placating customer service tone (for all my mom's talk of good manners, she could out-Karen the worst of them), and I hate that my current state warrants it. After an endless day of flight delays and cancellations, on what was supposed to have been a direct flight to Fairbanks, I am on the verge of a breakdown.

Forcing a smile, I blink away the frustration simmering behind my eyes and swallow the nausea from exhaustion. "Look," I glance at the name tag pinned to her sweatshirt, "Therèse. I made the reservation earlier this week. I have the confirmation email here, and another one from the Starlight Lodge earlier today. The check-in date is for today, Saturday December nineteenth, through Tuesday, December twenty-second." I take a deep breath as I point to the proof on my phone, trying to stay calm. "So I am struggling to understand why you have no record of my reservation. Or why you told me to find somewhere else to stay, instead of honoring the reservation I have proof of!" I grimace at the anger in my voice, rubbing my eyes to keep from crying. "My apologies, again, ma'am. I am calm, I promise you. It's just that I've been traveling since four in the morning. My flight was canceled, and I had two layovers from hell. And then it was damn near impossible to get an Uber who would drive me out this far, and if I can't stay here, I don't know how I'm going to get back to town, because it's almost midnight, and it's snowing, and I am so exhausted, I just want a hot shower and a good cry." It's a miracle that I manage to keep myself calm by end of my pitiable monologue.

Thank the stars the lobby is empty; if anyone saw me breaking down in front of Therèse like this, I would simply return to the airport and never come back, northern lights be damned. It's bad enough that this poor woman has to witness it in the first place.

Alaska is not what I expected. The brochure made it look glamorous. Heavy pine forest, snow-covered boughs, a luxurious geodesic dome cabin. Instead, the few spruce trees I could see in the dark are short, scraggly, and scrubby. While the nature lover in me firmly believes that all trees are beautiful, these ain't exactly inspiring any raptures in me.

Fairbanks feels like any generic suburb in America, instead of some picturesque, wild town in the interior of Alaska. Maybe it'd look different in the daylight, but my ride here was all streetlights and fast food signs. Not that I'll see much daylight while I'm here, about three hours a day is what the brochure said.

If I can't find a place to stay, I might end up back on a plane before I see daylight at all! An echo of my last visit home.

On top of every other dashed expectation, this "Starlight Lodge" is kind of a dump. The main office is run-down, the stained green carpets and shabby furniture perfumed with stale cigarette smoke. The rustic building looks as if someone DIYed the construction from scrap forty years ago, and never made a single improvement since.

From what I could see in the dark, the domes are pretty. About a dozen of them spread out around the main lodge, elevated on wooden platforms. The resort is walled-in with a scrap wood fence. Not exactly picturesque, or private. Out of the small windows of the lodge, I can barely make out the tent canvas hallways that connect the domes to the main building. Pallet-wood walls line the sides of the platforms, blocking the view of their neighbors. It looks like a strong wind could take down the whole compound.

"Look, baby," Therèse's accent deepens as she drops the customer service voice; almost instantly, I can breathe easier. "I wish I had a better answer for you. But you are not in our system, and we've been booked solid for weeks. I don't know why the website did you dirty, but it should not have let you make this reservation. We've got no availability, not even a cot to sleep on, because the owners' nephew is sleeping in the office while he's on break from school." She sighs, long nails tapping on the counter. "Look, I can get you a pillow and a blanket, let you sleep on the couch for the night. No taxi or Uber will be coming back up here this late."

I glance at the saggy futon in front of the smoldering fireplace. The disappointment is bitter, but I'm too exhausted to think, and too much of a realist to argue; there'd be no point to it, and I can figure out what to do after a few hours of shut-eye. "Honestly, I am so plumb tired that the couch would be heaven. Thank you."

"I'll let the owners know there's something broke on the website." Therèse fetches me a pillow and blanket from a storage closet. "They're on vacation, so hopefully they can fix it from Phoenix. Good thing it's the off-season, otherwise there'd be more unexpected guests."

The weight of my duffel bag on my shoulder again makes me wince; carrying it around all day is going to leave me hurting tomorrow too. If I'd done what I was supposed to do (planned this trip ahead of time), I would have brought a better suitcase. This is my punishment for being spontaneous: a sore back and a night on a shitty couch.

"Memphis?" I ask as she hands me a pillow and lumpy comforter.

"What's that?" Therèse asks.

"Your accent," I explain. "Are you from Memphis?"

She beams. "Good ear! My mama is, but I was born and raised in Oklahoma."

"I'm from near Asheville," I say, tossing the duffel next to the couch. Actually, I'm from nowhere near Asheville, but it's the only city most people recognize unless they're from the area. "What brings you up this far north?"

"My wife is stationed here. Army, career. Can't wait until she's transferred somewhere warmer!" Therèse says, that polite customer service tone back in her voice. I smile and nod, taking the hint to stop asking her personal questions. "My shift is ending in about ten minutes, and we don't have an overnight desk worker in the off-season, so you should have plenty of privacy in here until Gladys gets here to start on breakfast. If you need anything, knock on the office door to wake Alex up. I can't refund you, but file a claim on your bank card to get your money back. The owners won't give you no trouble."

"Much obliged, ma'am," I spread the comforter over the couch to make myself a nest. Just as I'm about to finally lie down, the back door opens with a creak and brings in a rush of frigid air.

"Sorry to bother you, Therèse," the other guest, one with a real reservation, asks in a polite tone. "I was wondering if you wouldn't mind heating up some tea before you leave for the night? I'm having a little trouble falling asleep, and chamomile might—Rory?"

I whirl around at the mention of my name.

Sanzhar stands next to the desk, a parka draped over his co-ordinated flannel pajama set, heavy duck boots unlaced on his feet. He gapes at me, pushing his glasses up. His hair is down, rumpled and messy; the ends of his black waves curl around his jaw. "What are you doing here?"

"What the fuck are *you* doing here?" I stammer out in retort. Stars have mercy, even his pajamas are stylish! This is the most unkempt I've ever seen this man, and my Power Rangers hoodie and wrinkled joggers still leave me a complete scrub in comparison.

"Just a quick weekend trip." He glances to the blanket and pillow on the couch, frowning so hard, lines form between his brows. "Are you...going to sleep *there*?"

I huff. Out of everyone in the world who could possibly be here to witness my utter humiliation, it's fucking *Sanzhar*. As if this day could get any worse.

"Little mix up with the system," Therèse explains, glancing between us and backing away slowly. "I'll put the kettle on for you."

Stepping toward me, Sanzhar mutters a thank you, his eyes still examining me as he frowns. I can't help but fidget; normally his thinking face is unfocused, but being the subject of his analytical gaze makes me hyperaware that I've become a problem he needs to solve. His chin tilts up as he cocks his head. "You never said you were coming here."

"You didn't either," I mutter, shoulders hunching. I never realized I was this much taller than him; have we ever stood this close before? I resist the urge to pull my hoodie up, instead shoving my hands into my pocket. "Kind of a last-minute decision on my part. Didn't you tell Bill you were gonna spend time with your family?"

"That's what he wanted to hear." He snorts, the glow from the firelight flickering across his light brown skin. "Hard to get a word in around Bill to correct him."

I pause, eyes narrowing. Sanzhar always acts so polite, going along with the buddy-buddy familiarity Bill puts on with everyone but me and Gina. Yet the edge in Sanzhar's tone is unmistakably bitter.

"Well," Sanzhar nods, as if I've said something he agrees with. He bends down to pick up my duffel bag, groaning as he hauls it onto his shoulder. "Geez, this is heavy. Come on then!"

"What?" I ask, reaching out to take my bag back.

"Don't tell Therèse that I'm complaining about anything, but that couch is awful." Sanzhar waves a dismissive hand at the futon, sidestepping my attempt to grab the strap. "You'll stay with me."

"Absolutely not!" I cry, embarrassment burning hot as I blink back tears, turning away so Sanzhar won't see. I'm worn so slap out, there's no fighting them. "I just wanted to see the damn northern lights!"

The universe must be conspiring against me, just as it has my whole life. My flight was canceled, I had to argue with the Uber driver to even get here, my reservation somehow doesn't exist, and the night sky has been completely clouded over by snow!

And now this smarmy jackass wants to add insult to injury by *rescuing* me? As if I would accept help from the man who has made my job more miserable than ever!

"I should have known this would go wrong," I murmur, my voice husky. "Why can't anything go fucking right for once?"

"Look, Rory," Sanzhar's voice quiets; I still as his hand tentatively rests on my shoulder. If he can tell that I lean into the warmth of his hand, he doesn't mention it. "I know you have every reason to hate me. I didn't know Bill was going to give me your project without talking to you first—"

"It's not *my* project," I bite out. "Obviously."

"It is," Sanzhar insists, his speech quiet and slow. "You sourced the client, you pitched the deal, drafted the project plan, got buy-in from all of our teams and theirs. This is absolutely your project. You've been leading this every step of the way, and we would not have won this deal without you. I'm sorry Bill doesn't value the work you do, but you deserve all the credit for this."

When he sighs, my tears lose the battle against gravity to roll hot down my cheeks. I never realized how much I needed someone to simply say that, to recognize how much fucking effort I've put into this company.

"So in good conscience, I cannot allow you to sleep on this sorry excuse for a couch in the lobby, when I have a king-sized bed with a stunning view. This is literally the least I can do. Because I should have said something, at any point since he first floated the idea, and I'm sorry I didn't."

I wipe my eyes on my hoodie before I turn back to him, though my face must be splotchy as hell. My mama always said I was an ugly crier, and the pity in Sanzhar's eyes confirms that hasn't changed. But a king-sized bed, even one shared with Sanzhar, sounds like heaven after the exhausting, uphill battle I've fought against the universe today. One night of good sleep would feel like a win, however small it might be. I swallow, sniffling before I mutter, "Fine."

Sanzhar's oval face lights up with a broad smile—crooked, goofy, and entirely unlike his polite work mask. "Really?"

"Sure," I huff, softening at his eagerness. As much as I resent him for all he represents, *Bill* is the source of my problems; Sanzhar's got no dog in that fight, and he's new to the company at that. His apology won't change nothing, but it's enough for me to set aside my pride. "Just for the night. I can figure out what to do after some shut-eye. I'll get out of your hair in the morning."

"Here's your tea, Mr. Tursyn," Therèse sets a metal thermos on the counter with a *thunk*. "I take it you two know each other?"

"Yes, we are colleagues!" Sanzhar says, still beaming like a fool. "Rory will be staying with me. Thank you for the tea, Therèse!" He points with his chin at the couch, whispering low enough that only I can hear him, "Bring the blanket. The dome is freezing!"

I gather the comforter, murmuring a thanks to Therèse, too. She simply winks at me, and my cheeks burn at the implication behind it. I figured since she'd casually mentioned a wife, that she'd clocked me as queer, but into *Sanzhar*? If she only knew how much *that* was not on the table. Face on fire, I follow his broad shoulders through the door into the canvas-covered walkway that leads to the domes.

Chapter Four

The rest of the Starlight Lodge seems just as rustic as the lobby. The canvas walls of the walkway snap in the howling wind. The peaked roof puffs in and out, like it's breathing with every gust. I have to tilt my head a little so it doesn't smack me in the face. The cold seeps through the walls, and I shiver, putting my hood up. I should have put my coat on, like Sanzhar, but my parka was already wrapped around the strap of my duffel when he swiped it.

Sanzhar leads me to a dome halfway down the hall. We climb up some wooden stairs that look more like a ladder, and through a trapdoor. My breath catches in my throat as I look up through the dome.

Snow swirls around us from all sides, the tiny flakes a flurry of movement in the night sky. Even the scrubby spruce trees look magical, their dark shapes rampant and reaching skyward, illuminated from the floodlight over the parking lot. Sanzhar was right; this view is stunning, even in the pitch-dark of night.

The pallet wood walls, that looked so shabby when the Uber dropped me off, seem perfectly sound in the low light of the woodstove, creating a sense of isolation. I know there is a lodge, eleven other cabins. I can see them over the walls, some glowing with fire or lamplight, some mere outlines in the dark. But it doesn't feel like anyone else in the world exists outside of this dome. It's just me and Sanzhar in this frozen bubble, with a king-sized bed taking up half the room.

Maybe I should be more worried about sharing a bed with the coworker I barely know and utterly loathe, but any concern I can muster is piddling at best. I have no clue if Sanzhar knows I'm trans, nor any reason to think he'd try anything untoward. Compared to all the other fellas at work, Sanzhar is always considerate and polite, which is practically sweet when it comes to working in tech.

I frown. My stars, that apology must have gone a long way; he's gone from the most aggravating guy at work to "sweet" in the span of mere minutes.

Dropping my bag on a chair, Sanzhar clears his throat. "Sorry, I need to close the door. They have a lot of rules for staying in the domes, to prevent animals from trying to get in here."

"Oh." I step to the side so he can close the trapdoor, bolting it shut. "What kind of animals?"

"Oh!" Sanzhar's mouth drops open, brow furrowed the way it does when he's thinking through a problem. "Well, I'd assumed Therèse meant mice, but I suppose this bolt is a little hefty for rodents. Bears, presumably?"

"Bears?" My eyebrows raise.

"We can ask about that tomorrow." Sanzhar waves a hand. "There's no food allowed in the domes, only beverages. So unless you have a rotisserie chicken in your bag, we should survive the night."

I snort. "Darn, I knew I left something behind on the plane!"

Eyes crinkling behind his glasses, Sanzhar smiles at me, that crooked, genuine one that makes my chest flutter.

I shift my weight to my other foot, suddenly hyperaware of how Sanzhar might be perceiving me. My awareness of my own self has increased drastically with T (on account of how I now *want* to be aware of my body), but when I get remotely anxious, the boy stink hits me like a truck; today has been nothing but one anxiety after another. Forget looking splotchy and tired—under this Blue Ranger hoodie, I reek. "What's the shower situation like?"

"Oh!" Sanzhar jumps up, gesturing towards a wood panel wall at the back of the dome, behind the woodstove. "The water is heated by the stove, so it lasts maybe ten minutes before the pressure and temperature drops, and you can't control it. Frankly, I thought even the hot water was lukewarm at best." Sanzhar shrugs, a slight sneer crooking his mustache. "I'm going to be honest with you, Rory. Please don't tell anyone who works here that I'm complaining, but the bathroom sucks. It's cold, mildewy, and the lightbulb is really loud. The towels are scratchy, and the shower is tiny. *I* barely fit in there." He eyes me up and down. "*You're* going to have a bad time."

"Oh." My five-ten height has never felt taller. "I'm sure I've had worse."

It's strange, hearing Sanzhar ramble on so much, seeing so many more of his mannerisms that he never shows at work. But I suppose he's seen more of the real me in the five minutes since Therèse handed me the comforter, including seeing me cry—something I try to hide from most people, even though I am quite the emotional fella. I hold the blanket out to him. "I'll shower quick, if that's okay. Took three planes to get here, and I'd hate to stink up your bed."

Sanzhar smiles again. "If you're tired and would rather sleep, you don't have to, but I appreciate the consideration."

We stand there, staring at each other a moment longer. I eventually duck past him to retrieve my bathroom bag and sleep clothes from my duffel.

Sanzhar hangs up his coat, kicks off his boots and dives under the covers. "I knew it'd be cold here, but not this cold!"

I frown, toeing off my own boots. The floor is a little chilly through my socks, but not enough to warrant that level of dramatics. "It's not so bad."

"You're kidding, right?" Sanzhar gasps, unscrewing the lid from the thermos. "I wasn't worried about having trouble sleeping, I just wanted tea to warm up!" He slurps loudly, sighing dreamily into the steam.

"Aren't you from Minnesota? Shouldn't this be normal to you?" I gesture to the snow still whirling around us. The snow here isn't like it is in Minnesota, which is all fluffy flakes and heavy accumulation. The powder here is crystalline, shiny and sharp, forming flurries against the dark clouds. Part of me is disappointed that this is the only night I get in this dome, and it's cloudy. The rest of me is just in awe that this is real, that I'm here. It took me months to build up the courage to follow my partners to Minnesota, and yet I'm in fucking *Alaska* on a whim?

"I grew up in Huntsville, actually. I went to Minnesota for college, stuck around." Sanzhar snorts. "Car wouldn't start."

I chuckle politely. Not because that's a terrible joke, but because I'm low-key mad I didn't think of it. I love bad jokes. "You don't sound like you're from Alabama." My small-town ass has felt so out of place since moving to Minneapolis; I always clock the Southerners the second they open their mouths. There's no hint of accent in his tone, other than perhaps the slower cadence.

"Sorry, never picked up a Southern drawl," Sanzhar smiles into his tea. "My mom is from Seattle originally, and I went to a private school with an international program. I was born there, I grew up there, but most locals would agree with me that I'm not *from* there. It's kind of like Minnesota that way. I've lived in Minneapolis for over a decade now, and I'm still not *really* a Minnesotan."

"I get that. Hard to make real friends here. Er, there." I nod, shifting uncomfortably as I hold my bathroom stuff. Are we talking? Or should I just dip to go shower? I'm not sure what the rules are for making small talk with your work rival in a remote cabin that's basically a reverse snow globe. "Welp," I say, borrowing one of Bill's phrases to end an awkward meeting as I grab some shorts and a tee (because it really isn't *that* cold in here). "Shower."

Sanzhar nods, blissfully sipping his tea, bundled in the blankets.

The shower is as awful as promised. The thin plastic shower curtain clings to me, and I have to duck to wash my face and hair. I shower quickly, but still barely finish before the water slows to an ice cold trickle. I don't understand how mildew can grow in this ice box, but it stinks of mold, and the towels are disturbingly stiff.

By the time I'm in my sleep shorts and tee, I'm shivering. I should have listened to Sanzhar; it is fucking freezing in here.

Sanzhar smiles sympathetically as I dive under the covers. I typically would find an outlet, charge my phone, check for any messages from my partners. But I am cold and tired as all get out; they can wait until morning. They're all visiting their respective families for the holidays already anyway, so I'm not expecting anything other than some affectionate shit-talking about taking a spontaneous vacation without inviting anyone, and their well-meaning messages about how they miss me.

It'd mean more if I'd been invited to join any of them, but I get it. It's not that I wouldn't be welcome, but it'd invite invasive questions. We're already queer; bringing a "friend" home to meet their parents, when they're happily married or just moved in together, would lead to uncomfortable conversations. I've always been the third wheel in my triad since we first got together six years ago, and now I'm the fifth wheel of our polycule. Not only am I used to this, I asked for it; I'm not really a "meet the family" person. But things have been tense since The Rupture in the polycule, and it's hard to know where I'm welcome or not. It'd be nice to be invited, to know I'm still wanted.

"Thank you," I murmur to Sanzhar, as the fire in the woodstove pops. The snow has slowed a bit, but the sky is still an endless blanket of dark clouds. No stars, let alone an aurora. The blankets rustle in the quiet as I settle in, careful to stay on my side of the bed.

"I'm glad I happened to want tea," Sanzhar sighs, snuggling into his pillows with a quiet, pleased huff as he shifts to look at me. "You said this was a last-minute trip?"

"Yeah," I sigh. "I just wanted a break. From everything. After...you know."

Sanzhar hums in acknowledgment, sucking his teeth awkwardly. "Sorry. Again."

"Not your fault. Besides, I've always wanted to see the northern lights, ever since I was a kid." Unsure of how vulnerable I can be with the coworker I barely know, I adjust the pillow behind me, eyes trained on the sky. "Back when I wanted to be an astronaut. And while I gave up on *that* dream, I still like astronomy. And what kind of amateur astronomer am I, who has never seen an aurora borealis?" I snort. "A southern one, I reckon. I was hoping there might be some chance in Minneapolis, but without a car, I'd have to get real lucky to see them. Downside of living downtown."

Sanzhar is quiet, and I can feel his eyes examining me. He looks away as soon as I glance to his side of the bed, clearing his throat. "How did you find out about this place?"

I shrug. "Brochure in the breakroom."

"Really?" Sanzhar perks up, beaming at me with that crooked smile. "That was mine! Oh, this worked out better than I expected!"

With a snort, I ask, "Were you hoping for a travel buddy?"

"Was I hoping that someone would see it and decide to take a spontaneous flight to Fairbanks for the solstice in a fit of totally justified anger?" Sanzhar chuckles. "No, I just wanted someone to *ask* about it. To spark a conversation and connect with someone, person to person for once. I was looking for a change, taking this job. Some career growth, a new direction. But the culture there, it's..." His smile fades.

"Lonely?" I prompt.

"Yeah." Sanzhar nods, looking at his tea. "No one talks to each other, except you and Gina. Like, Bill talks. He talks all the fucking time!" He rolls his eyes.

I snort; maybe we can find some common ground after all. "Never says shit, though."

"Exactly!" Sanzhar smiles again, and my chest warms a little. "All anyone talks about is just business and social politics, and I haven't found anyone there I connect with yet. Gina's nice, but I totally get why she doesn't want to be buddy-buddy with many people there."

"Well, now you have me." The words slip out unexpectedly, like they're rote and rehearsed. But that wasn't manners; for once, I meant it. "I won't lie, I definitely resented you. Until you said...what you said in the lobby. There's no fixing the situation, but it helps that you think I'm right to be upset about it." My fingers tighten around the pillow, and I fight for control over the tremor in my voice. I've already cried in front of him; I refuse to do it again. Damn Cancer moon. "Like you said, there's a lot of politics in the office, and Bill likes to play favorites. Part of the reason he doesn't like *me* is because I don't play his games. I try to be nice to everybody, even the folks on Bill's shit list, and Bill don't like that." I chuckle, a little sardonic. "Which is why I'm always on his shit list."

There are other reasons of course, but that's the only one I have any control over. I just don't see the point in being rude to my coworkers, just to make him hate me a little less. He's gonna hate me either way.

"I'd like that. If we can be friends." Setting the tea on the bedside table, Sanzhar settles into his pillow, smiling.

I smile back, blinking heavily as drowsiness overcomes me. "You'll have to become friends with Gina, too. We're a package deal."

"Good. She's funny." He bites his lip, rolling onto his back. "She's part of the reason I took this job."

My stomach tenses in dread. Oh stars, is Sanzhar in Gina's creepy fan club?

"I came in for the interview, and she was decorating for Pride," he explains hesitantly. "I thought that might mean the office was accepting of diversity."

"Oh, baby, no," I laugh, nestling further into the blankets. Is Sanzhar queer, or is he simply referring to the fact that he's the only Asian fella on a team of white men? He's never hinted at being gay, bi, or even straight, one way or another. Still, I'm relieved he didn't take this job for a chance with Gina. "She does that as a reminder for everybody leering at her all day that she's gay. Nothing really stops them, though."

"Gross," Sanzhar groans, that slight sneer back on his face. The glow from the woodstove catches the shadow of his curling lip. "The creepy attention, not her being gay!" he adds in a rush.

"I figured," I chuckle. "Bill don't do shit about it, and start-up culture hasn't really caught on to having an HR department." I shrug. "The point is, you don't have to play his games. I get if you want to—it'll make your job a lot easier! But you can challenge him. He hates when he's wrong, but he doesn't have the technical knowledge we do."

"Thanks, Rory," Sanzhar murmurs, setting his glasses on the side table. His eyes, bigger without the thick lenses, meet mine in the low light. "Even though I contributed to everything sucking so hard that you had to run away to Alaska, I'm glad you're here."

I smile, sleep overtaking me with every gust of wind and swirl of snow outside, every pop of the woodstove. "Me too. I was mostly pissed because you're the only other person there who could actually handle the technicalities of the project, but it helps to know that you didn't want it. That it was one of Bill's games, probably pitting us against each other."

"I'll talk to him. Once we're back," Sanzhar murmurs, but I'm too exhausted to respond. I fall asleep just as he adds quietly, "I promise."

Sunday

Chapter Five

The sky is still dark when I wake up, and the wind gusts blow snow all around in swirls of crystals that *tink* against the glass. However, I am no longer cold. In fact, any grogginess evaporates as I take in just how flushed and hot I am.

Cold? A scoff escapes me at the very idea. How could I possibly be cold when Sanzhar is wrapped around me like a goddamn body pillow?

I must have been worn slap out, because I have zero recollection of becoming the little spoon in the middle of the night. Nor when Sanzhar's arm wrapped around my middle, hand splayed across my sternum. Or when his face nestled between my shoulder blades, his deep breaths steady and warm through my shirt. I especially do not recall waking up when his knee slipped between mine, or when our legs entangled under the pile of blankets.

My dick is *throbbing* against Sanzhar's thigh. Testosterone has blessed me with incredibly affirming bottom growth, but right now I am eternally grateful that my dick is nowhere big enough for Sanzhar to notice in his sleep.

Squeezing my eyes shut, I try to get a hold of myself, to slow my shallow breath before any embarrassing sounds can escape. I cannot grind on fucking Sanzhar Tursyn's leg! We're already far past the point of professionalism. Unintentional spooning at night does not necessarily constitute sexual harassment; humping his leg definitely would!

I don't know nothing about his sexuality, I don't know if he's even single, and I do not know if he'd be into me! Yesterday, the idea of wanting anything remotely sexual with Sanzhar would have been laughable.

Are my standards really so low, that an apology and a favor can make me forget the many, *many* reasons I should not want this? Want him?

Sanzhar shifts in his sleep, his massive arm pulling me in tighter.

Standards who?

I swallow the whimper that tickles my throat. My partners wouldn't mind if anything happened; we've always been open, even if I'm the only one in our polycule still hooking up with other people from time to time. There'd be no harm—

No! While Sanhzar and I might have become tentative friends yesterday, I should not hook up with him. He still has my project, that would get messy, and I don't rightly know if I'm attracted to him like that, or if I'm simply horny enough to be very tempted right now.

However, it is very apparent that this surge of early-morning lust is one-sided. Sanzhar is pressed against me from face to knees; if his cock was hard too, I would feel it, and I don't. With that reminder to prevent any rash decisions, I shift my hips a smidge, just enough to get Sanzhar's leg out of direct contact with my crotch, before he wakes up and things get awkward for both of us.

Even that bare movement is too much, apparently, because he grumbles into my back, "Stop moving."

I snort; I had thought he was dead asleep. "Look, it's one thing for you to use me as a body pillow. It's another to tell me what to do."

"Oh." Sanzhar stiffens, but doesn't pull away. "Good morning, Rory." His voice is thick with sleep, and I love how my name sounds in his quiet, slow murmur. My boxers must be flooded at this point. "Sorry, I didn't think to warn you that I have a tendency to sleep-snuggle. This usually only happens with close friends. Is this okay?"

My heart melts at the vulnerability in his voice—the slight hitch of hesitation in his question, despite the fact that he hasn't pulled away at all. If he's not queer, he's incredibly secure in his sexuality. "Yeah, this is okay."

He smiles against my back, and the rest of me melts, too. The ache between my thighs rears up again at the consent, amidst the quiet intimacy of the moment. I half expect his hand to roam, the way many people's would in a moment like this.

But Sanzhar simply relaxes against me with a quiet sigh, the same, pleased little huff he made last night as he settled under the covers. I never expected the polite, reserved Sanzhar to be so affectionate. So endearing. So comfortable to be around—Fuck, I cannot start crushing on Sanzhar!

Being a polyamorous Libra can be a curse as much as a blessing; setting aside my long-standing resentment should not be this easy. And yet, the Sanzhar holding me in Alaska is not the quiet, aloof Sanzhar who never pushes back against Bill. Hopefully, this inconvenient crush goes away once we're back to normal.

"What time is it?" I ask. The sky outside of the dome is pitch-dark; even the floodlights from the lodge are off. The fire in the stove has burned down to a few sparse coals, barely casting a red glow. It's so quiet here. Only the wind and the sound of our breath, and the two of us wrapped around each other under the pile of blankets. I burrow deeper into the warmth, resting my hand over Sanzhar's so he keeps it pressed against my chest.

"I imagine around seven, but it's hard to say without getting my phone. Therèse said it starts getting lighter around eight or nine, but I feel well rested." Sanzhar smiles again. "Is there a pressing appointment you have today? Or is my speculation enough?"

I chuckle, but my throat gets tight. "I should get up, find another place to stay. Hopefully, I can still see the borealis while I'm here." I swallow, disappointment leaking into the comfortable warm bubble of Sanzhar's arms. "Else I'll figure out my flight back home."

Sanzhar's hand flexes against my chest. "Why not stay here?"

"What?" I look over my shoulder, only seeing the tangled mess of Sanzhar's bedhead poking out from the blankets. "Why, I couldn't! Letting me stay here one night is already too much."

"I would like it, if you stayed." Sanzhar tilts his head back, and my world narrows to his brown, sleep-filled eyes looking at me from under the comforter. "I would appreciate the company." He smiles, the crooked grin mischievous. "Also, I wouldn't mind having someone else to light the woodstove in the mornings."

Laughter bubbles out of me, and I roll onto my back. Sanzhar's hand, his leg, his body stay pressed against me, adjusting as I move. "Oh, is that so? I'm invited to stay, but only if I do manual labor? Do I need to haul the wood in? Go full lumberjack and split it with an axe, too?"

"I'm sure the staff would appreciate the help, but no, just lighting it." Sanzhar fights his grin. "That way I don't have to get out of bed until it's warm. Even the thought of getting up right now makes me want to cry. I hate being cold."

"You live in Minnesota?" I tsk. "And took a vacation to *Alaska* in December?"

"The experience is worth the discomfort," Sanzhar shrugs, burrowing himself under my arm so he can lay his head on my shoulder.

Tucking my arm around him, I still don't quite understand how we became this comfortable so fast. But I can't imagine pulling away, not now when I know how his broad shoulders and soft belly feel against me. Once again, I find myself wishing his hand would move towards a nipple, or down under my shorts, where I'm soaking wet. But his hand remains still, other than the one fingertip absentmindedly twirling the hair on my chest. The slow trail of his touch is so intimate that I don't dare move, in case he doesn't realize he's doing it, because I don't want him to stop. Other than my partners, I've rarely found myself craving someone's touch as much as I need Sanzhar's right now.

"And I meant it. I would like the company. I've never seen them either, the northern lights. We could experience that together." He pauses, biting his lip. "I travel by myself so often, see so many things, it'd be nice to share that with a friend, for once. Especially when it'd be so special for you."

My eyes flick up to the overcast sky, where the snow-thick clouds are barely starting to lighten from black to midnight blue. "Do you think we will? See them?"

"Only one way to find out," Sanzhar murmurs. "Does that mean you'll stay?"

If Sanzhar knew how drastically my feelings about him had switched from loathing to lust in the last twelve hours, he might not want me to. But I can't imagine saying no when this lonely, affectionate nerd is practically begging for my company. With a heavy swallow, I nod. "I reckon so."

"Good!" Sanzhar hugs me tight, his enthusiastic wiggle making me smile with him. "Once it gets a bit lighter—and warmer, if you light the stove—we can venture to the lobby for breakfast before we need to get ready for the daylight excursion."

I snort. "Oh, okay. You've got the whole day planned already."

"Oh, not me!" Sanzhar waves a hand. "They do all the planning for us! After breakfast, we're going skiing."

"What?" With a yelp, I try to sit up, but Sanzhar pushes me back down. "Oh my stars! No! I don't ski. There is no physical coordination in this body!"

"It's just cross-country, you'll be fine." He pats my chest, as if placating me. "Therèse talked me into it, and if I can do it, you can do it. Besides, I already paid for all of the excursions, and it's the same price for one or two people."

"Sanzhar, I—" I freeze as his brown eyes flick up to me again, the slightest pout on his lips. I would never have expected this much affection, eagerness, or assertive enthusiasm from the quiet, demure man who keeps to himself around the office. It's like he's a whole different person. Maybe he has been lonely, working there. I sigh, because even with my partners' support, I know loneliness, especially this time of year. If he travels alone, and works alone, and is presumably single, I could help ease the ache a little bit. "I can't guarantee I'll be any good, but I will try. Just don't laugh at just how much of a klutz I am."

Sanzhar beams, hugging me again. "This trip is going to be amazing!"

I smile back, already dreading how my three hours of daylight will go. But like Sanzhar said, the experience would be worth the discomfort.

Chapter Six

The discomfort is worse than I expected. We just started, but so far? Not worth it.

Panting, I choke on frigid air as I try to catch my breath. Ahead of me, the line of a half dozen other guests braving the cold, led by the trail guide named Alex, ascend a small rise between the pines. I shouldn't stop; I'm already falling behind. But the second I start to pizza my skis up the small incline again, the way Alex demonstrated so easily during our lesson, another coughing fit seizes my lungs.

The sound is hoarse, and Sanzhar looks back at me with a concerned wince. "Are you okay?" he calls, already halfway up the hill.

"I'll catch up!" I call back, the sound more of a loud whisper. Fuck the cold, I hate this. I don't miss North Carolina enough to move back, but the climate there never gave me asthma. This particular side effect of exercising only started happening in Minneapolis, whenever there's a polar vortex—whatever the fuck that is.

Skis pizzaed carefully on the hill, Sanzhar levels a skeptical look at me over his shoulder. "We barely started!" He gestures behind me, where a dozen domes sparkle in the clear, bright sunlight a mere fifty feet away.

Considering we're only getting a few hours of sunlight, I should be grateful the snow clouds have cleared. Except I didn't bring sunglasses. Sun dogs form a triple sun on the horizon, and the snow is so bright, my eyes hurt.

"I normally don't do cardio in the cold," I huff, hoping Sanzhar hears me despite my wheezing. My chest feels like it's splitting in half. Even though I lift weights four days a week, attempting to ascend a barely there incline with skis strapped to my feet is exerting myself beyond comfort. "My Southern ass is not built for ten-degree weather."

Sanzhar turns back to the rest of the group, then looks at the lodge, and back at me. He nods to himself before calling, "Look out below!" His ski pizza turns to French fries, and his arms wave comically as he slides, ever so slowly, backward down the small hill.

It has to be a record for the slowest ski crash known to humankind. Barely keeping my skis under myself, I watch helplessly as he collides directly into me. Snow crunches as his skis nudge mine. For a second, I think that's it, that our skis will merely bump at the bottom of the hill, with barely a wobble between us.

But then, the end of my ski hooks under his. As if in slow motion, we both topple sideways in a tangle of skis, poles, and limbs into the powdery snow.

"You were supposed to move out of the way!" Sanzhar wheezes, his whole body shaking against mine. His elbow digs into my stomach, his ski pole wedged between us. The end of one of my skis is stuck in the snow, propping my leg up midair. Sanzhar's are criss-crossed over it.

"I can barely breathe, let alone move in these things!" I protest, my hip aching. Despite my grumpy tone, my smile is irrepressible with Sanzhar's quiet giggles. "You expect me to jump sideways? What part of 'klutz' didn't you get?"

"You two okay down there?" The guide calls from the top of the hill. Alex is a young Alaska Native guy—Athabascan, specifically—who introduced himself as "the Starlight Lodge owners' nephew, crashing here for winter break" at the start of his skiing demonstration. He easily glides down the rise to us, braking with a spray of powder. He expertly frees Sanzhar's and my boots from the skis with quick pops of his pole to the latches, and holds out a hand. "Everyone okay? Anything hurt?"

"Just my dignity," Sanzhar takes it, allowing Alex to help him up, but then winces when he stands. "And maybe my ankle."

"Can you put weight on it?" Alex asks, catching him before Sanzhar can fall.

I scramble to my feet, my hand finding Sanzhar's to help support his weight. I half expect him to shrug me off, but he simply tucks his arm through mine.

Gingerly, Sanzhar puts his foot down. "I think so? It doesn't feel like a sprain, just twisted."

"You want to try to ski it off?" Alex asks, frowning when Sanzhar keeps his weight off of it. He swings his backpack around, unzipping a pocket to pull out a first aid kit. "Or should we all head back?"

"Oh, no!" Sanzhar gestures for him to put the first aid kit away. "The group doesn't need to turn back!" he insists—to my disappointment, because *I* want to head back. "I can just go back on my own! I should be okay! I'll just walk slow."

"I can help!" I volunteer quickly. "I'll be sad to miss the skiing," a lie, "but I can walk with you, to make sure you get back okay."

Alex shakes his head. "No, we have to go back together. It's not safe to split up like this."

I frown, pointing to the lodge fifty feet away. "We're going just right there."

"And what will you do, if you see a bear?" Alex asks. "Leave him to get mauled?"

"Bear?" I yelp. Every boulder, every shadow under the spruce trees has suddenly become a hulking mass of fur and teeth. "Wouldn't we see it if it was this close?"

"Shouldn't they be hibernating?" Sanzhar asks, far more skeptical than me. I'm worried about getting eaten, and he's analyzing the seasonal habits of the wildlife.

"You never know! Sometimes they wake up, and they get hungry!" Alex huffs. "Look, I know it may not seem logical, but I'm not supposed to split up the group. The insurance company wouldn't like it! And even though it's pretty warm today—"

"It's ten degrees!" I mutter. Sanzhar snorts quietly.

"...there's still a risk of hypothermia and frostbite if I keep everyone out here too long." Alex winces. "Unc will get mad, because I already got us a bad review for arguing with a guest about climate change."

"We won't argue!" I insist, putting on my sweetest Southern charm, my friendly smile secretive as if Alex and I are co-conspirators. "We will leave a glowing review, and mention you by name! Rave about how knowledgeable and safety-oriented you are."

"You have an extra can of bear spray, right?" Sanzhar asks. "If bears are the risk, we can take that with us, for the insurance company's peace of mind. You wouldn't want to risk the other guests leaving a bad review because their ski trip was cut short."

Alex frowns. "Fine, but if he gets mauled by a bear, you still have to write the review."

"Five out of five stars, Alex. Even if Sanzhar gets eaten." I put my hand to my chest. "Scout's honor."

"Why are we so sure *I'd* get eaten? *You* can't even breathe right now," Sanzhar muses, then smiles when I elbow him and nod in Alex's direction. "Oh yes, regardless, whoever survives will leave a glowing review!"

Handing Sanzhar one of the aerosol cans from his bag, Alex skis up the hill as easily as if he's taking a stroll in the park to rejoin the other guests; they all seem to be handling the dry cold better than I could ever hope to.

"Is your ankle actually hurt?" I ask Sanzhar, hefting the skis under one arm so I can take his elbow again. "Or were you faking for my sake?"

"I was planning on faking a twisted ankle for *my* sake," Sanzhar says with a teasing smile. "But the prophecy fulfilled itself, and I actually did twist my ankle a bit. Could I have kept going? Sure. But you can't breathe, and I'm cold as fuck."

"Stars, imagine Bill hearing you talk like that," I tsk, melting at the way he leans into my touch, as if he actually wants my help. "Such language."

"I used you as a heating pad last night, Rory," Sanzhar winks, and my body blazes. I would not be surprised if my face is steaming. Sanzhar can use me for whatever the hell he wants. "I think we're well into the cuss words territory of familiarity."

He takes my poles from me, and sets off toward the lodge, exaggerating the limp for show, in case anyone is watching. Though most of the guests are already skiing through the scrubby spruce trees.

I scramble to catch up with him, my boots falling through the crust on the snow with every step. He lets me take his arm again when I do. Even if we never see the aurora while we're here, this will be an adventure to remember. In the daylight, the wilderness surrounding us is strikingly beautiful—rugged yet pristine in the isolation of this little valley against the mountainside. My pessimistic impression from last night feels mean-spirited now that I can see the sweeping vistas of snow and mountains, with trees and endless blue skies around us.

My chest starts to ache again, and I adjust the skis under my arms. Stunning as it is, I'd rather admire the scenery from inside.

Chapter Seven

If someone had told me twenty-four hours ago (right after that awful meeting), that today I'd be in Alaska, sitting in front of a crackling fire, sipping mulled wine in the fading twilight, with Sanzhar's feet adorned in moon phase socks in my lap, I would have laughed in their face. If they'd even so much as hinted that I'd wish it was in any way romantic, I would have smacked them. Not hard, but still—they'd get smacked.

Yet, here I am, wishing this was a date. Sanzhar's hair is down; the long, silky waves curl around his chin. He grins at me with a mischievous smirk every time his peg passes mine on the cribbage board balanced on his knees, as if goading me into reacting.

One leg folded under me in the middle of the saggy couch, I can't help but lean toward him, drinking in the details I've never noticed before. Like the small mole near his ear, how he gently smooths his mustache after each sip of wine, or the outline of amber around his pupil where the honey gold melts into dark brown.

"Your crib," Sanzhar reminds me, smiling over his mug of mulled wine as he catches me staring for too long.

"Oh, right," I jump, glancing at the cards, trying to remember how to count. "Fifteen two, fifteen four, and a pair is six."

"Can I ask you something?" he asks as I move my peg, just two spots ahead of him. "About how...*out* you are, at work? About your transition, I mean."

My chest tightens, and I can't help but glance around. For the twilight excursion, most of the guests went into town to the natural history museum. The rest are spending some alone time in their domes. The room is empty, except for us and Gladys, the old white lady who runs catering and room service, currently snoring in a nearby recliner.

Therèse quietly told us to let Gladys feed us, but if we actually needed room service or anything, come to her instead. Her tone implied it wasn't entirely out of concern for this elderly woman, but more of a question of her housekeeping competency. The muttered, "ol' biddy needs to retire already," under her breath as she walked away just solidified it. Considering Therèse is currently washing the lunch dishes while Gladys is passed out, I understand her frustration. Though Gladys was very sweet before she dozed off, getting Sanzhar an ice pack and cooing, "I know exactly what you two need!" before she added a nip of brandy to our mulled wine.

It's just the three of us in the lobby, so I murmur, "Not that I try *that* hard to pass, but is it that obvious?"

Taking the cards from me to shuffle the deck, Sanzhar shakes his head, lips parting and brow furrowing. His thinking face. I know it so well, but I've never witnessed this quiet concentration in the dim firelight before. Not with the flush of wine on his cheeks, or his hair loose and looking irresistibly soft. "Bill mentioned it early on, which I thought was odd, especially considering you've never brought it up once in the whole time

I've worked here." My heart sinks; Bill outed me to a complete stranger? And so quickly? But Sanzhar smirks, and I am desperate to hear what he's about to say. "Like, I probably would have figured it out from the Blahaj plushie on your desk—"

Laughter bursts out of me, surprising me because the hurt and anger is already stewing in my gut. "Oh my stars, you got my number!"

Sanzhar's expression softens a bit. "But he told me pretty much right away, the same week I started. Sorry, if I'd known you didn't want it to be common knowledge, I would have said something to him. At first, I thought he'd heard some things about me through the rumor mill, and he wanted to make me feel welcome. But the longer time went on, and he showed his true colors, I think Bill was trying to warn me to stay away from you." He winces. "I hope it's obvious that his plan backfired, because I think it's cool that you're trans." Sanzhar frowns, lines deepening between his eyebrows. "Well, not that it's cool *that* you're trans. That came out wrong. I think you're cool, and your gender has nothing to do with it. I mean, it does, because obviously being trans is important to who you are, but it's not important to me—no, that's still wrong. I think you're cool, and I'm going to leave it at that."

"Damn it all," I sigh as Sanzhar rambles, resigned disappointment heavy on my chest. Sanzhar was the first new hire after me, so maybe Bill thought he was doing the right thing by letting Sanzhar know when everyone else does? But that is something he should have asked first, before outing me to my new coworker. That was definitely covered in the resources I shared with the office when I announced I was transitioning, but it's been three years. Maybe he'd forgotten?

Had Bill even read them?

Squeezing my eyes shut to fight the tears threatening to form, I shake my head, fully aware I'm making excuses for him in an attempt to delude myself, so I don't get angry. So I can go back to work on Wednesday, without leaving my notice on Bill's desk to find when he comes back in the New Year. I've known Bill had trouble with the pronouns, but I thought he'd finally gotten the message from Gina correcting him. That or the visual difference after three years on testosterone and top surgery. Apparently, he's only putting on a show in front of Gina and I, when in reality, my boss is outing me and misgendering me behind my back to the rest of the office.

I hate feeling so vulnerable. I'm proud to be trans, but I *have* to be careful about when and to whom I disclose that. This is my life, my livelihood that Bill is so casually endangering to god knows who. "I can't afford to lose this job," I mutter to myself, attempting to quell my outrage and disappointment with that bitter reminder.

"Can't you?"

I jump; I plumb forgot Sanzhar is close enough to hear that.

He looks at me, head cocked slightly. "Why *this* job?"

"I—" I pause, wondering which of the many reasons I want to share.

Sanzhar already knows I'm trans, and doesn't seem to have a problem with me. Both of his feet are still resting on my thigh (even though only one was hurting earlier). He still deals the cards on his lap, passing me my stack.

I organize them absentmindedly, passing him an ace and an eight for his crib, that hopefully won't give him too many points. Quietly, I admit, "I don't really have a safety net. I have enough savings to last me a few months, but that's it. And I don't want to do just anything, you know? I want to work in aerospace engineering, but it's hard to find jobs these days. And my odds of getting a government position are zip, and I can't just move anywhere—"

"Why not?" Sanzhar asks as we lay our cards down to peg up. "You're incredibly competent. Anyone with a brain would hire you in an instant."

I snort. It should be obvious. "Uh...trans? Even if the government was hiring for desk jobs, they're not about to hire a trans guy. I can't enlist in the military—not that I'd want to! And there are very few places left in this country where my basic rights are protected." I move my peg to tie with Sanzhar, who picks his cards up. "Kind of important to me. And that's not even going into finding a company whose values I respect, or who aren't sending all of their engineering jobs overseas."

"Fifteen two, fifteen four, fifteen six, a pair is eight, and a run is eleven, another run is fourteen." Sanzhar's smirk is less mischievous this time, even though that hand brings him one point away from a win. His brows furrow as he looks at his mug.

I move my peg up for the pair of fours in my hand, then nod for him to go.

He flashes me a pair of aces with a shrug. "That's game. Wanna go again?"

I shake my head, unsure of what to say now.

Equally quiet, Sanzhar sips his wine, humming quietly in satisfaction as his thumb runs over his mustache. Just like he did with his morning coffee, and the tomato soup with lunch. I wonder if he does it at work, too. I'll have to pay attention next time he makes himself an afternoon tea. I smile, my mood brightening ever so slightly. At least that's something to look forward to at work. I have another friend there now.

"I hate that place," Sanzhar says out of the blue, staring hard at the star anise floating in his wine. "Everyone at work. The job. The clients. Bill."

I rest my hand on his uninjured ankle, waiting. I wish I was more surprised, but now that I've seen the Sanzhar I've come to know over the last day, the quiet, polite recluse at work is not the real him. He's been miserable, too.

"I met Bill at some industry conference last spring, and he convinced me that I was wasting my time there, that I would flourish in a start-up, all of this *bullshit*," Sanzhar frowns. "I can't believe I bought it."

"He's good at running his mouth," I murmur, my thumb tracing the bone of his ankle through his sock. "Don't say shit, but he's very good at convincing everyone of the complete nothing he's saying."

"Exactly," Sanzhar's eyes flick down to my hand on his ankle, then up to mine. My heart thumps in my chest. "My old job misses me. They've offered me a raise, and they let go of the person who was making my job miserable. And I miss them."

"Then why not go?" As if I'm back outside, my chest aches at the suggestion, cold and hollow and cracking in half. I scold myself; I do not know this man well enough for him to be triggering my abandonment issues. I sip my wine to hide whatever my face might be doing, letting the cozy spices and citrus warm me from the inside out.

Sanzhar takes a slow sip, eyes meeting mine over the brim of our mugs. "I guess I don't want to believe it'll stay this bad. My mom always said to keep a job for a year, to give it a chance. I want it to get better, so I'm going to stick it out a while longer." He smiles at me, that crooked grin sending my stomach fluttering. "Besides, it *is* getting better! I have a friend at work now, and he's a sweetheart."

My cheeks burn as my whole body flushes. When I open my mouth to reply, I choke on my spit, biting my tongue in the process of trying to form words.

Sanzhar laughs. "Though I have to say, he's not the wittiest conversationalist."

"Hush your mouth!" I smack his ankle. My cheeks are probably heating the lodge better than the fire is. I might cause the tundra to melt from my embarrassment alone.

"Hey, careful! I'm injured!" Sanzhar grins.

"You hurt your other ankle, you liar," I tease.

Sanzhar bats his eyelashes innocently. "The brandy cured me."

"Who was making your job miserable?" I ask. Stars, that is an awful way to change the subject. A pang of guilt strikes my chest as Sanzhar's smile falls into a grimace. "Apologies, you don't have to answer that! How much wine have I had?"

He chuckles. "It's okay. This one guy I worked with ended up being a mutual friend of a...*friend*," I raise my eyebrows; that pause tells me everything I need to know, "outside of work. Except he was the ex of said mutual friend, so he felt threatened by me for some reason."

"For some reason?" I tease.

"It's not what you think." Sanzhar shakes his head. "I'm pretty open about being ace in queer circles—"

"You're ace? Like asexual?" My embarrassment plunges from burning hot to freezing cold, like I ran outside and dove naked into a snowbank. Stars, I have really been reading this wrong.

Part of me wants to pull away, give him space, respect the nonsexual boundary he just subtly set. Had he been picking up on my unexpected-yet-overwhelming crush that exploded into existence this morning? Is that why he told me? Or is that just what Sanzhar tells his friends? Is this touchy affection we've been exchanging how he is with everybody? If I pull away now, will that signal that I was only touchy because I'm into him in a way he's not comfortable with?

Despite the humiliation churning in my gut, I keep my hand on his ankle and my body turned toward him. Because I do want to be his friend, even if my chest aches because he just rejected me in the nicest way possible.

"Yeah, asexual, aromantic, agender, all of the A's. Before you ask, he/him pronouns, and I consider myself cis and agender. I don't really subscribe to any sex, gender, relationship, et cetera, norms. I'm just me." Sanzhar shrugs, thankfully not picking up on my wounded crush, or my internal panic on how to handle it. "But this coworker *thought* his ex was into me. The ex and I met at a thrift store, and ended up becoming shopping buddies. He invited me to hang out with his friends from time to time, but we were never that close. Our friendship was never anything but platonic, at least not that I picked up on." Sanzhar's face falls. My hand tightens around my mug; I just want to talk to this douche canoe who hurt him. "Anyway, my esteemed colleague started telling everyone that I have erectile dysfunction, low testosterone, that I can't get it up, all of this extremely unprofessional and inappropriate stuff! Which, not that it matters, isn't even true!" He tsks, shrugging in a way that is anything but casual. "My libido is perfectly average."

"What the fuck?" I say, too loudly, because Gladys jerks awake for a few seconds before falling back asleep. Even Therèse pokes her head out of the kitchen, before disappearing again. I lower my voice, "What the fuck?"

Sanzhar snorts. "Yeah. Of all the ace stereotypes, spreading rumors of a medical condition is probably the least professional option. Like, at least make a joke about me being a celibate, Asian nerd," he rolls his eyes, settling back against the arm of the couch.

"I'm sorry that happened to you." I squeeze his ankle. "You didn't deserve that."

"Thank you, Rory." Sanzhar smiles, hugging his mug to his chest. "I know that, but it's nice to hear. So yeah, between that going down, and Bill stroking my ego with weekly emails of complete bullshit, I decided to leave." He tilts his head ever so slightly, examining me carefully. "Still don't know if it was the right call, but I'm starting to feel optimistic."

I smile. Even if I'm nursing a bruised crush, I'm glad we're friends. I can get over these silly feelings, if it means a genuine friendship with Sanzhar. My crush probably only feels so overwhelming because we're here, alone together, instead of in our real lives. This side of him has shown me just how unhappy Sanzhar is at work, and I am determined to make him smile and laugh and banter with me when we get back. Work has been awful for both of us, but together, maybe it will get better.

Chapter Eight

Now that I've had sleep and food, and time to settle into the dome, I'm taking my woodstove responsibilities very seriously. I've adjusted the airflow per the Internet's recommendations, so the dome is now toasty warm. Sanzhar only has the blankets up to his chest, instead of over his head like he had this morning. My Charizard lounge pants and Baby Yoda tee are enough to keep me warm as I sprawl on top of the covers, staring up at the stars through the dome ceiling. Frost blooms into intricate white lace in the corners of the plexiglass, a natural frame for the night sky and crescent moon.

It's odd, hanging out in the dome when neither of us is especially tired. But it's been dark for hours, and there's nowhere else to sit except the giant bed, so we've been hanging out in our pajamas all evening. There's a tension that wasn't there this morning. We're both sticking to our own side of the bed, and despite our day of easy conversation, we're awkwardly quiet.

Maybe it's all in my head? Maybe I'm causing the tension? Maybe Sanzhar is just giving me space, worried about being too much when we barely know each other. Or maybe it's because I'm on top of the covers, and *I'm* keeping us from cuddling? Is he hurt and confused too?

To keep from fretting more than I already am, I pull out my phone to check the aurora forecast for the millionth time in the past hour, decidedly ignoring the group chat with my partners. They were collectively confused by my spontaneous vacation, and everyone reacted exactly how I expected they would: Dawn was glad I'm taking time off work for once, Charlie was entertained by the travel misfortunes that led me here (once xe confirmed I'm safe), Ducky pretended to be offended that I didn't invite them, and Sarah asked me to bring her a Toblerone from the airport.

The chat is now back to the subject of their trips to see their families—Sarah and Dawn are on their way to Vermont for their first Christmas as newlyweds with Sarah's new in-laws, and Ducky is bringing Charlie back home to North Carolina to introduce xim to their parents. I need to check out of the "happy family holiday season" conversation for a bit for my own peace of mind, and focus on why I'm here: the northern lights.

A nervous frisson buzzes under my skin, one that feels a bit too much like anxiety for comfort. How will I feel, to finally see it? Disappointed at how uneventful it is, like when I landed in Fairbanks to essentially find a normal town? Overwhelmed by the magnitude, like when I returned to the polycule's empty house on Christmas day two years ago, after my family kicked me out? Solace, like...

I frown, unsure of a time in my life when I ever felt at peace. Like when I first moved to Minneapolis, I suppose. When Sarah and Ducky picked me up from the airport and brought me to the messy, loud house they used to share with Dawn and Charlie, two friends who would eventually join our polycule. The home I would eventually move out of when that mess, that noise, that peace became tense and uncomfortable and heavy. It helped, moving out before The Rupture; who knows where I'd be if I hadn't found a place of my own?

With a shake of my head, I set an alarm for when the odds of a visible borealis are highest, though the forums tell me that my chances are lower compared to most days. I grumble, setting another for a handful of other expected peaks. Who needs sleep? I am here to see a damn aurora, and if I miss it, I already know I'll be kicking myself.

"Everything okay?" Sanzhar's question makes me practically jump out of my skin, despite the gentle tone of his voice. He chuckles, the sound quiet. "Sorry, didn't mean to scare you."

"Nah, I was just checking the forecast." I wave the phone, smiling apologetically.

"Therèse has us on the wake-up list, if it starts." Sanzhar rolls on his side toward me, brown eyes wide without his glasses.

"But what if it starts after her shift ends?" My chest tightens just thinking about it, and I check the early morning hours again.

"Then Alex will call us."

"What if Alex don't wake up?"

Sanzhar exhales slowly. "Are you going to stay up, then?"

I shrug. "I don't want to miss it."

He nods, burrowing under the blanket.

"You want me to wake you, if it starts?"

The bed shakes with his quiet laughter. "Yes, thank you. Good night, Rory."

"Night," I murmur, uneasy at the finality in his tone. But I look back up at the night sky, cold and clear and stunningly beautiful. I'm not tired in the least, tension running through my jittering legs...

A piercing ring jolts me awake.

I blink, struggling to understand where I am, and full of panic about what the noise is.

It takes Sanzhar snapping at me to "shut that damn thing off!" to make me realize my alarm is screaming, somewhere under the pillow. I scramble for a long moment to find it and fumble with the slide to turn it off.

"Apologies," I whisper once the alarm is silenced, the echo of the annoying chime ringing in the dome. I would be less sorry if there was an aurora, but no, the only light in the clear sky is the stars.

Sanzhar grumbles, "Is that going to happen again?"

I wince. "Maybe a few times."

After a heavy sigh, Sanzhar demands, "Tell me about your family."

"What the fuck?" I laugh at the unexpected question.

"You said earlier that you didn't have a safety net. Let's start there. I'm assuming that your transition might have something to do with it. Yes, or no?" Sanzhar practically snaps.

"You sure you want to know, Tursyn?" I tease, a little waspish. Who the hell does he think he is, asking questions like that? "You sound like you want to talk about something else."

"Okay, fine, *Callahan*, you just woke me up from a very deep sleep!" Sanzhar pulls the blanket down from his face, his scowl undermined completely by his bedhead. "I am a heavy sleeper, I do not appreciate being woken up, and you just told me you were planning on doing it several more times tonight." He sighs, eyes squeezing shut like the very idea pains him. "And while I do not particularly like you much at this very moment, I liked you earlier when we were talking about our lives. So in an attempt to keep myself from sending you outside to get eaten by bears, tell me about your damn family!"

"Yes," I blurt out, doubting he's serious about kicking me out, but it still strikes like a blow to my chest.

"Yes, what?" Sanzhar prompts.

"Yes, they were not happy about my transition," I mutter quietly. "We're not really in contact."

Sanzhar frowns, squinting in the dark. His features are barely visible in the dim glow from the woodstove. "I'm sorry. I should have asked about something easier. Or lighter. Or not anything at all. That was just the first thing I thought of, and now I feel like an ass." His hand snakes out from under the covers, tracing the thin skin of my inner arm to find my hand in the dark. I open my fingers to take his hand, ignoring the goose bumps rising along my skin that his fingertips leave in their wake. "Do you want to talk about it?"

I want to say no, to keep my heart safe from remembering how it felt. But part of me is reassured by his apology, and strangely, something deep inside me wants to. With my partners, I avoid the subject; Sarah's family kicked her out in high school and she doesn't handle the subject well, and Ducky gets enraged on our behalf. I spend more time calming them down than processing my own feelings. If Sanzhar is asking, if he wants to know...

"Can... Can you go first?" I ask, embarrassed by my hesitancy. "I will tell you—I *want* to tell you, I just need to ease into the conversation. Can you tell me about your family?"

"There's not much to tell," Sanzhar murmurs, scooting closer across the bed until our palms align and our fingers fit together comfortably. "My mom used to work as a geologist for NASA, back in the nineties."

"Oh my stars, that's so cool!" I blurt out.

"It was the best time of her life," he murmurs. "Until they sent her to Alabama, where she met my dad. He was a cosmonaut-in-training from Kazakhstan, stationed there for training exercises."

"'There's not much to tell,'" I mock. "Not much to tell, my ass! Your dad was a cosmonaut, and your mom worked for NASA, right after the Cold War? Classic tale of star-crossed lovers!"

"Don't get too excited, I'm not done yet," Sanzhar teases. "Besides, I don't think he ever went up, just was a candidate in the training program. Anyway, they hit it off, she fell in love, believed everything he said about their future together, got pregnant with me. He was so happy, picked out my name, helped paint the nursery, everything." He scoffs. "And then he went back to his wife and kids that she didn't know about in Astana. He offered to take me with him to raise me with his family instead, but Mom wanted to keep me, and we never heard from him again.

"NASA fired her for performance issues before I was one. She believes, understandably, that she was fired for having a child out of wedlock, she just couldn't prove it." His hand tightens around mine. "So she took a teaching job at a university in Huntsville, got tenure, and stayed there, because she wanted me to have stability. She was a good mom, just...distant. I can't really blame her. Raising a child on her own in Alabama was not the life she envisioned for herself."

I roll onto my side, leaving mere inches of space and a blanket between us. His breath is warm against my collarbone. "You didn't ask to be born. As the parent, she should have stepped up for you."

"She did what she could," Sanzhar's tone turns defensive, "I never wanted for anything. She taught me what was important in life. I got to travel with her to academic conferences or research trips, which sparked my own interest in science. If I ever need her, she'd be there for me. Would she charge me rent if I moved in with her? Absolutely!" he concedes with a chuckle. "But she chose me, when she could have let my dad take me back to Kazakhstan and left the whole situation in her past. She stepped up for me in all the ways she could, and then some."

The affection in his voice tells me I might be projecting, or perhaps more used to comforting my partners than listening. There seems to be genuine love between him and his mom, just not the same love Sarah or I experienced, conditional as it was.

"But yeah, like I said, she was just a bit distant. I'm not supposed to know this, but I was diagnosed with autism when

I was a kid. Mom never told me, but my guidance counselor let it slip. From my mom's viewpoint, I'm perfectly neurotypical, probably because she's on the spectrum, too. Only we're a bit different, in how we experience it. I'm more talkative than she is, more social. Like how I'm so affectionate." He holds up our joined hands. "She hated being touched, and I just...I crave it. Always have."

I resist the urge to kiss the back of his hand, to cover him in love and affection to make up for what he's been missing; he literally just reiterated that we're friends, and only friends. "Do you talk to her often?"

Sanzhar shrugs. "A few times a year. Birthdays, mostly. We send each other pictures though, of whatever we're up to in the world."

"Have you sent her any from here?"

He pauses. "I haven't taken any yet."

"Something to do tomorrow," I murmur, wishing I could do the same for my family. But the ball's been in their court since they told me to leave. I sent them all an email a few days after I got home from that disaster of a Christmas, telling them I was open to being a part of their lives in whatever capacity they wanted. Only my younger brother responded, reiterating that they expected an apology and his sister back, before I would be welcome home.

Sanzhar nods. "Your turn. If you're up for it."

I huff, because even thinking about my brother makes my chest ache. "Will you actually kick me out to get eaten by bears if I don't?"

"Of course not!" he cries, as if offended by the suggestion, burying his face into my shoulder. "After I practically had to beg on my knees last night just to get you to stay? Besides, they're hibernating!"

I blink, trying to mask my reaction to the visual of Sanzhar on his knees, those brown eyes pleading and hands gripping my hips, even as my heart pounds. Fortunately, figuring out where to start talking about my family cools my ardor.

"My family was pretty normal," I murmur. "Middle class, Christmas and Easter Christians when I was growing up, all of that. My parents always made sure we were well-behaved, got good grades, volunteered in the community." I shrug. This part is the easy part, and yet my heart preemptively aches. "I was definitely the middle child in the family, not as successful as my older sister, not as popular as my younger brother. But they still loved me, were proud of me getting my master's. They looked the other way when I brought my partners around, so long as we all pretended we were just friends."

"That sounds like the bare minimum," Sanzhar teases.

"Hey, I would take the bare minimum at this point." I snort. "I transitioned when I moved to Minnesota. I'd known for a while I was a guy, so I took the new state and job as an opportunity to reinvent myself. My partners were supportive, so it felt like the right time." I smile, remembering how optimistic and delusional I'd been, to believe that my family would come around. That my triad would stay strong enough to replace them until they did. "I told my parents that I was transitioning, but I don't think they quite believed me. Or perhaps they thought it would be another part of my life they could ignore. But by the time I went home for Christmas two years ago, my voice had dropped, I'd had top surgery, and I was starting to grow a beard."

"How'd they react?"

I shake my head, eyes burning at the memory of the horrified expression on my sister's face when she looked at me, the tears in my mother's eyes. We'd never been close; in hindsight, that sisterhood and mother-daughter bond I'd always felt was missing was probably because I was never her sister, nor my mother's daughter. "It could have been worse. It could have been *better*, but it could have been worse. My dad told me it was best if I left, and we haven't talked since. My brother sent me a few texts asking me to apologize to everyone—"

"For what?" Sanzhar snaps.

"Exactly." I huff, angry all over again thanks to Sanzhar validating my feelings. "He was just trying to keep the peace, but he was trying to keep *their* peace, not mine. So I never did, and no one ever reached out again."

"I'm sorry," Sanzhar murmurs, his thumb strokes mine. "You—"

My phone alarm splits through the air; we both jump in panic.

"I swear to god, Rory, I am about to chuck that phone into the fire!" Sanzhar groans, burying his head under the pillows.

I spew out apologies as I shut the sound off.

"Can you please choose a different ringtone?" Sanzhar begs. "That is sensory hell, Rory! Set it to vibrate? Better yet, turn it off? We have nowhere to be, we don't need alarms!"

"But the aurora—"

Sanzhar's pillow smacks me in the face. "Therèse will call us!"

I sputter in shocked laughter. I would never in a million years have expected the polite, sweet Sanzhar to resort to pillow-fighting. Before this, the angriest I'd ever seen him was mild annoyance when someone stole his lunch from the breakroom fridge. "You did not just do that!"

"I did, and I'll do it again, Callahan!" Sanzhar smirks, sitting up with his pillow aloft, ready to strike again. "Turn the damn alarm off! I hate it! It's like a fork scraping a plate!"

If he's going to be juvenile enough for a pillow fight, I can show him the middle child tactics he missed out on as an only child. With a grin, I feint like I'm going for his pillow, only to grab him around the waist and tickle him when he raises it out of reach.

Sanzhar shrieks, thrashing to escape my grasp. But I have him pinned facedown between my legs in seconds. His pillow is long forgotten as my fingers find the spots along his torso where he's most sensitive.

"I'm sorry! I give up!" he pleads, hands gripping my wrists to stop me.

I let him think he's overpowered me. "You're not gonna hit me with the pillow again?"

"No!"

"Or kick me out to get eaten by bears?"

"No! I promise!"

"Or throw my phone in the fire?"

His silence speaks volumes. I break free of Sanzhar's grip on my wrists with ease, until he's pleading with me again before I've even touched him.

"I promise! Your phone is safe!" Sanzhar manages to roll around, so he's looking up at me. His long hair is sprawled against the mattress, eyes bright with laughter. "As long as you promise to change the alarm."

As I look down at him, my heart pounds in my throat, and in my dick. Despite that undercurrent of anxiety—telling me that I can't miss my chance, that I have to stay awake, to check the forecast again—I only have eyes for Sanzhar, looking up at me and asking for something so simple that will make him happy. I nod, unable to speak.

Am I alone in this? This moment is another one I refuse to pass up, but I don't know if Sanzhar wants what I do.

"Rory?" Sanzhar asks, his voice husky. "You said that you have—"

An uncanny wail makes us both jump. Adrenaline humming through my veins, I scramble off of Sanzhar, who sits up. His arm loops through mine as we squint into the dark outside.

Another wail echoes, then another, until a dozen howls are harmonizing in the night.

"Wolves?" Sanzhar asks, clinging to me. The blanket has become a tangled mess around our legs. "Oh my god, are we about to see actual wolves?! Rory!" he squeals.

I train my eyes on the woods around us, looking for any sign of them. “There!”

A rime gray blur emerges from the spruce trees, followed by a few others, patches of light fur barely visible in the dark. A few of them step close enough to the main building that the floodlights flick on, exposing half a dozen wolves in the glow. Their tails swishing, the wolf pack circles past the lodge along the rise, keeping their distance, but lingering long enough for us to relax into awed silence.

“This is amazing,” Sanzhar murmurs, his hand leaving my side to yank the blanket back over us. Curling up around each other, we settle against the headboard, our maybe-sexually charged moment forgotten. This is a thrilling new sight to see together, a magical moment we can share.

Soaking in the wolves singing to us, I quiet the alarms on my phone for Sanzhar. I want to stay up—to keep checking over and over, to ease this anxiety, to simply have a win, even one as symbolic as seeing the northern lights—but Sanzhar doesn’t want to share in my manic obsession, so I will let him sleep. We’re in this adventure together, and that means being considerate of his needs. Just like how he’s not making me give up, I shouldn’t drag him along with me.

By the time the wolves leave, Sanzhar is asleep in my arms, his breath deep and even. The skies are still a riot of stars, clear and sharp, and without a hint of an aurora. As the forecast confirms my odds for the rest of the night are low, I swallow my disappointment that another night will pass without seeing them. I still set a couple more alarms, just in case. Tomorrow is our last chance, our last night together before returning to our real lives. There’s still a small hope, and I can’t help but cling to that.

I settle against Sanzhar, smiling as he grumbles and clings to me harder. The faintest purse of his lips presses against my chest. Before I can talk myself out of the delusional hope alighting my body, I kiss the crown of his head, murmuring a quiet "good night".

Monday

Chapter Nine

Sanzhar sets a steaming cup of coffee in front of me. "Here. Gladys just made a fresh pot."

Eyes bleary and dry from exhaustion, I blink up at him, swallowing the bite of syrup-coated pancake in my mouth, before muttering a "thanks."

"Yeah, well, you look like you need it." Sitting down across the small table from me, Sanzhar sips his own coffee. The circles under his eyes mirror my own.

We've barely spoken a word since we walked in. The rest of the guests have been chattering on about the wolves at the communal dining table. Without a single word of discussion, Sanzhar loaded up a tray with our breakfasts, and I followed him with our first cups of coffee. He claimed a table for two in the corner, out of earshot from everyone, and away from the bright lights over the long table. Which I appreciate; with how wore out I am, I would be miserable company for anyone but the equally tired Sanzhar.

Outside, the sky is just starting to lighten into civil twilight—a sign that breakfast will be ending soon. The three-hour time difference and three hours of daylight are really fucking with my internal clock. It's almost ten, but my body feels like it's lunchtime, and my brain is wondering why I'm up before dawn.

Anxiety led me to set my alarm a few more times, and despite my best efforts, Sanzhar woke every time, albeit less grumpily with the quieter ringtone. I wasted my sleep, and his, and for what? The wolves were lovely, but I could have slept all night and not missed anything once they'd left. It was just cold and dark, my anxiety was obnoxious, and I utterly failed at being considerate to this sweet guy, who is actively trying to be my friend.

"About last night," Sanzhar sighs, his face twisted into a wince. "Can I ask—"

"Yes, I am so sorry!" I groan, rubbing my forehead. "I feel like the biggest jackass on the planet."

"Oh." Sanzhar's face falls. Not the reaction I expected.

"I will be better behaved tonight!" I take his hand over the table. Brows furrowed, he frowns at the way my fingers wrap around his palm. Sanzhar doesn't pull away, but he doesn't take my hand either. My stomach drops. He literally told me how important his sleep is to him, and I completely disregarded the bare minimum he was asking for. "No more alarms, I promise!"

Sanzhar blinks at me. "What?"

Feeling like the rudest, most inconsiderate fuckup on this green earth, I shake my head, sliding my hand off of his. He don't want me touching him, so I wrap it around the ceramic mug instead. We woke up spooning again this morning, but that doesn't mean he wants to be openly affectionate with another man in front of everybody else. "I can't guarantee I won't be an anxious wreck again, but I promise I will do everything I can to make sure I don't bother you none. I'll have my phone off completely, I swear!"

"You think I'm upset at you for waking me up?" Sanzhar's mustache twitches, and a quiet chuckle escapes him. "Rory, I don't care about that. Yeah, I was not the happiest camper last night, but I understand. We're here for an experience of a lifetime, you don't want to miss it."

"You're not mad at me?" My hand tightens around the coffee mug, almost painfully hot against my skin.

"No, Rory, I'm not." Sanzhar gestures for my hand back. I give it to him, cheeks burning as he laces our fingers together. "I honestly appreciate that you were so diligent in checking. I slept better knowing you'd wake me if there was something to see." The smile he gives me is the reserved one Sanzhar wears at work. I hate that he feels the need to placate me. "How about this? We're already sleep-deprived and jet-lagged. Why don't we fuck up our sleep schedules more? Sleep this afternoon, so we can stay awake when it's the darkest? The weather forecast looks clear again tonight, and the aurora forecast looks promising."

"You wanna skip the excursions?" I ask, skeptical. "I thought you were excited about the hot springs."

"Oh, we are *not* skipping the hot springs!" Sanzhar scoffs at the suggestion. "You think *I'm* going to pass up the chance for a soak in scalding hot water? We are absolutely going!" His smile goes the tiniest bit crooked, and my chest loosens in relief. "No, I'm suggesting we ask Gladys to make us dinner a bit early, so we can sleep through the *twilight* excursion." He waves a hand. "It's just some Christmas market in town. The only part I'd enjoy there would be the mulled wine, which Gladys will have here anyway."

"No Christmas spirit, Tursyn?" I tease, blowing on my coffee before taking a sip. Not even scalding hot caffeine can make me more alert.

With the faintest eye roll, Sanzhar shakes his head. "Born and raised atheist. For me, Christmas has always been just another day."

"No presents or nothing growing up?" I ask, thinking of my own family. The hollow in my chest aches as I remember the joy, the nostalgia, the memories, forever tainted by their prejudice. "No quirky family traditions, or singing, or a special dinner? Nothing?"

Sanzhar shakes his head.

I hate to pry into his personal affairs, but I ask anyway, "Did you ever feel you were missing out as a kid?"

"Not really," Sanzhar shrugs. "Never had anything to compare it to. Mom would give me gifts for New Year's, so I wouldn't feel left out about presents after winter break was over. But now, the only tradition I carry on is marathoning Lord of the Rings and eating junk food."

"Extended version?" I smirk, dragging my finger up his palm, all the while questioning if I should. But he seems fine with affection, so maybe a little platonic flirting is within his comfort zone. Or maybe I'm setting myself up for heartache once we're back to normal, and we're not on hand-holding terms anymore.

Fighting a smile, Sanzhar scoffs. "Of course."

"Sounds way better than going to church, like I had to as a kid." I snort. Sounds better than being alone and in my feelings, which is what I'm fixing to do later this week. I don't miss the presents, or the food, or the singing; I just miss the company.

Like she has the past two years, Sarah is going skiing with Dawn's family in Vermont, but this Christmas is their first as a married couple. Charlie and Ducky will be in North Carolina until New Year's Eve. For the past two years, Charlie brought Ducky along to xir parents' house in Wisconsin, but this year Mama Duck insisted on finally meeting Charlie.

Ducky said I could come along, but we all unspokenly knew it'd be only as a friend. The rumors would fly like a bat out of hell if anyone in our hometown found out Ducky, Sarah, and I are all polyamorous, so I decided to stay home. The ache would be worse, being in town that long and not seeing my family, all while pretending I'm just friends with Charlie and Ducky, instead of their partner.

"Do you approve of my plan?" Sanzhar interrupts my memories, his question almost shy. His fingertips tease mine. Is he flirting back? Or is this more platonic affection? "It is the solstice today. There's a certain poetry to staying up on the longest night of the year."

I grin, touched by his support after how inconsiderate I was the night before. "Poetry? That's not very cynical atheist of you."

"Oh yes, because heathens have no whimsy." He snorts. "I'll get right on that sonnet about the axial tilt. The real reason for the season!"

We chuckle together, hands still entangled as we pick at our breakfast. Chiding myself for reading too much into a bit of hand-holding, I eat more of my pancakes before murmuring, "Thank you. For letting me stay with you, and the plan, and all of it."

Sanzhar shakes his head, his brows furrowing slightly. "I tend to be a bit of a solitary creature. It's nice, far better than I could have imagined, sharing this experience with you." His brown eyes flick up to mine, making my breath catch in my throat. "I don't want our last opportunity to pass us by."

I swallow, my throat strangely tight for so early in the morning. "Can't never could, right?"

Sanzhar beams, then leans in all secretive-like. "Can you, uh...sweet-talk Gladys? I asked her if it was possible for us to have dinner early, and she did not seem thrilled about the idea. But she's making spaghetti tonight, and I saw garlic bread was on the menu, and you may not know this about me yet, but I *love* garlic bread. You're better at turning on the charm than I am."

"Garlic bread, huh?" I tease. "And you came after my Blahaj? Who's the stereotype now?"

Sanzhar presses a hand to his chest. "The bond between an ace person and their garlic bread is sacred."

"I'll see what I can do," I grin. Sanzhar is not giving himself nearly enough credit in the charming department. I'll make him garlic bread myself if I have to. "So, if you weren't going to yell at me for how rude my alarms were, what were you going to say earlier?"

Sanzhar gapes helplessly before clearing his throat. "Oh, uh, nothing!"

Narrowing my eyes, I cock my head to the side. "Seemed real serious for nothing."

Squirming in his chair, Sanzhar winces. "I was wondering, if you don't mind me asking...um, you've mentioned that you have partners. I just want to check that they're okay, with you sharing a bed, and spooning with your coworker?" His eyes go wide, and he waves the hand that isn't holding mine. "Not suggesting anything untoward is happening of course, just want to make sure I'm not crossing any boundaries. Personally or professionally! Because you are kind of a people pleaser, and I'm not sure that you would say anything if I was overstepping."

Delight blooms in my chest. While I *wish* that something untoward was happening, his frantic babbling is cute. Normally, Sanzhar keeps his thoughts inside, until he's analyzed every possibility and has everything coherently laid out and ready to explain.

He holds up our hands, rocking a bit as he rambles anxiously, "Like, is this okay with you? And anyone else you might be involved with? I don't know if I'm asking the right questions. Maybe you're not exclusive with anyone, or you're polyamorous, or something. But I realized last night that we hadn't really discussed boundaries, and there's no HR for me to consult, or any company policy for running into your coworker on vacation and sharing a bed, and I just want to make sure we're cool."

I bite my lip to hide my grin, utterly failing as soon as I open my mouth to put him out of his misery. My cheeks burn from how wide my smile is. "Sanzhar. We're cool."

"Oh, good, you were taking a long time to respond!" He practically sags in relief.

"I am polyamorous, and my partners and I are not exclusive," I explain. "So no one is going to mind us spooning."

Sanzhar tilts his head. "And what does that mean for you? What does that look like?"

I huff a quiet laugh at how quickly his thinking face has snapped into place now that he's got something to ponder. "I have three partners and a metamour. Three of us—Sarah, Ducky and I—formed a triad about five years ago. They moved to Minnesota first, and I joined them once I found a job." Reaching the harder part of our history always makes my gut clench. My hand tightens around Sanzhar's as I fuss with my pancakes. "Since then, Sarah started seeing Dawn, who owns the house we all lived in. And our other roommate Charlie joined our triad to become a quad. I got a little claustrophobic in all that, so I moved out to get more alone time. And eventually, that led to everyone pairing off, and our polycule is more of a vee-shape now?" I wince, wondering if I'm clinging to a hopeless situation because I don't want to lose the only family I have left. "Basically, Sarah married her now-wife, my metamour, Dawn. And the other two took that shift harder than I did, since they were all living together, and I had already found a place of my own. Ducky and Charlie wound up moving out of Dawn's house. They stayed nesting partners, but they both ended things with Sarah. So I am the only bond still holding everyone together."

Taking a long sip of coffee, Sanzhar goes deep in thinking mode, his frown forming lines between his eyebrows.

"Yeah, it got messy, you don't need to follow the specifics." I snort. "Long story short, I don't need their approval to do nothing, except form a permanent fluid bond, or bring a new person over to theirs. Easier for me, since I live alone, but they run into that problem with their respective nesting partners."

"Fluid bond?" Sanzhar asks, examining a piece of reindeer sausage, before tentatively biting into it.

"That can mean different things for different people. For us, that means if I want to forgo protection with someone on an ongoing basis." I pause. I'm not sure how much detail Sanzhar wants, if he even wants to talk about the specifics, or if he's more on the sex-repulsed side of the ace spectrum. "I spent most of my life understanding myself to be a masc lesbian, until my late twenties, so all of my partners are sapphic women or non-binary folk. They've all supported my transition from the start, and they love me as the bi man I am today. They just want me to be safe, since I tend to uh...date around more than them. So either use protection, exchange health info every time, or stick to hand stuff. If something turns serious, that rule can ease up a bit, they just want to know about the change in advance."

Nodding, Sanzhar hums knowingly around the sausage in his mouth.

"They'd welcome anyone I want to start a relationship with into the polycule, of course. Even now, when they're no longer in a relationship with each other." I snort. "It's kind of like divorced parents who have a kid together, trying to reassure me that it's not my fault they got divorced, and they love me no matter what, except I'm sleeping with three of them." At Sanzhar's disturbed look, I laugh. "Sorry, that metaphor got away from me. We're still family, is what I'm saying, even if the romance ain't there for everybody anymore. Sure, shit got complicated, but we've all been there for each other as much as we can."

"As an aroace person, I would find this a tad overwhelming," Sanzhar teases. "But it sounds really nice, having so many people to be close with like that."

"Sanzhar, I'm fucking polyamorous, and *I* find it overwhelming. All the time! That's why I moved out!" I meet his smile, my heart skipping a beat at the soft look he's giving me. I shouldn't hope, not when Sanzhar literally just implied he wants no part of it—or when he hasn't indicated that he's open to *any* relationships, especially not messy, polyamorous ones.

However, I can't help but think he would get along with everyone. Sanzhar seems like he'd be into board games, so Charlie and him would be besties in no time. And I can picture Dawn sitting him down for a heart-to-heart, or Sarah experimenting with new cake recipes for him to try. Ducky...well, Ducky is an acquired taste for even the most patient people, but they'd probably figure it out eventually. And Sanzhar basically just asked me if I'm available. Fretted all night, in fact, if he *should* ask, so maybe hoping ain't as hopeless as I'm telling myself.

I huff as I take the last bite of my pancakes, chiding myself *again* for reading too much into it. Typical—one ambiguous conversation, and I'm planning our future. A future of board games and baking, but still, that is as much of a future as I typically want in a relationship.

"Good morning, Starlight Lodge!"

Sanzhar and I jump. The quiet murmur of the dining area that's been insulating our deeply personal conversation goes silent.

Near the door, Alex has his deer hide mittens cupped around his mouth. His fur lined parka is bundled around him so tightly that only his youthful face is visible. "The van to Chena Hot Springs leaves in fifteen minutes. There are locker rooms there that cost fifty cents. Grab your swimsuits, towels, flip-flops, and quarters, and let's go!"

"And put your dishes in the bins!" Gladys calls from the kitchen.

I lean in close to Sanzhar, grinning all mischievous-like. "Get my swimsuit and a towel for me? I'm fixing to butter Gladys up, help with the dishes a bit."

"Good man, Rory," Sanzhar beams, giving my hand one last squeeze. "If she happens to offer extra garlic bread, the answer is yes."

I laugh as he scurries through the back door to the domes. If he wants us to stay up all night for the mere hope of seeing the aurora, I'll do my part. Even if Sanzhar doesn't want me the way I want him, I'm glad we're friends. There's no one else I'd rather share the longest night of the year with.

Chapter Ten

I should have changed at the dome. The locker rooms at the hot springs are...as rustic as the resort we're staying at. They're clean enough—they smell better than the bathroom at our dome, at least. There are shower stalls for changing and rinsing off before we get in the springs, though most of the men at our resort are stripping in front of their lockers. But I am reluctant to disrobe; there's only a thin plastic sheet between me and a potential hate crime, depending on who checks to see if the shower is available. I hate to cut into our limited hot spring time, but safety first.

Sanzhar seems to hesitate, too, glancing at me. "Do you want to take turns?" he murmurs. "Stand guard for each other?"

"Oh my stars, yes, please!" I sigh in relief, though I suspect he's suggesting this purely for my sake. Still, I'm touched by his consideration.

"You go first," Sanzhar nods. "That way I can run right from the shower to the water."

"Freeze baby," I tease, dipping behind the shower curtain. Despite the heat registers in the locker room, the air is frigid. I'm shivering by the time I've showered, and get my trunks on. The thin hotel towel around my shoulders, and the worn flip-flops between my toes and the floor, don't do anything to help.

The locker room is mostly empty by the time Sanzhar has changed and showered, too. Audibly shivering, he scurries past me, tossing his towel and clothes to me, no hint of limp from his twisted ankle yesterday. All I see is a quick flash of bare, light brown skin. The tantalizing glimpse of his thick waist and broad shoulders is enough to make my mouth water after two nights of unsatisfied arousal. "You got quarters, right?" he calls over his shoulder before disappearing outside. "Fuck, I'm so cold!"

I laugh as I lock up our stuff, our phones on the pile of clothes in the locker, Sanzhar's glasses carefully balanced on top. Service on the drive here was spotty, so our phones are both off to save battery. Because I am utterly hopeless, the sight of our belongings commingled in the locker, his glasses cushioned by my hat, makes my heart glow with delusional warmth.

Until I exit the locker room, when cold air punches me in the chest. I manage to maintain a little more dignity than I did skiing yesterday as I approach the steaming pool, lined with boulders. The air smells of sulfur, though I'm sure the view will be lovely—once I can appreciate it from the water. Right now, everything hurts. I shuffle as quickly as I can towards the water, full of tourists relaxing up to their necks.

Sanzhar waves at me from the edge of the crowd, chatting with Alex near the railing. It's weird to see Alex out of outdoor gear, but like Sanzhar, he's up to his neck; his thin shoulders are barely visible through the mineral water. Dropping our towels on a chair, I carefully descend into the delightfully hot pool, sighing with relief when my ice cold feet start to thaw.

Both of them are staring, their eyes on my chest. I resist the urge to cover myself, incredibly self-conscious until the water is finally deep enough to cover my scars. I'm not ashamed of them. But while I haven't picked up on any blatant prejudice from anyone at our resort to make me *that* nervous, having people stare at them so closely is always awkward.

"Trans guy, huh?" Alex nods approvingly as I join them, the warm water embracing my limbs as I slowly glide along. His hair, pulled up in a topknot to stay dry, is longer than I expected now that it's not tucked under his hat and parka. "My older brother too."

"Oh!" I exclaim, the tension of their stares finally easing. I was starting to worry that maybe I should have done more research into how trans-friendly the Athabascan community is.

"His boyfriend is a drag queen down in Anchorage. He's fucking hilarious! I dunno how that dork pulled someone so cool!" Alex perks up, looking boyishly youthful as always. "If you guys ever come back in the summer, hit me up, I'll get you into one of her shows. Look her up on social media—Aurora Holealis!"

"Oh, we will!" I have never wanted to see a drag show more. "Sanzhar, we're coming back in the summer, right?" I turn to him, expecting him to smile and join in.

Except Sanzhar is still staring at me, his expression lost in that frowning pout that tells me he's deep in thought. Usually, his eyes would be unfocused as he analyzes whatever is processing in his pretty head; right now, they are zeroed in on my chest.

"Sanzhar?" I prompt. Worry starts to creep in that I've overstepped somehow by suggesting we'll travel here again in the future.

"Hot," is all he says, more to himself than to me. "Oh no."

I frown. How long has he been in the water? "Is the heat getting to you?"

Sanzhar blinks, jaw snapping shut as he looks up at me. "How much do you work out?" He says it with a frown, as if demanding an explanation.

"What? Oh!" My face burns, and it has nothing to do with the steamy water. Did he just call *me* hot? I look down at my chest, self-consciously touching the scars under my pecs. "Oh my stars!"

"Oh no," Sanzhar mutters again, slipping under the water. Bubbles surface in the spot where he was just standing.

I shoot Alex a panicked look. "Is he okay?"

With a shrug, Alex backs away toward another group of guests. "I'll uh...go. Feeling like a third wheel."

"What?" I ask, yet again, just as Sanzhar resurfaces with a groan, smoothing his long hair back. My heart skips a beat as he wipes the water from his eyes. His smooth tan skin glows as steam rises from him. With his hair slicked back, his parted lips glossy from the water, and those big brown eyes blinking at me, my mouth goes dry.

Oh my stars, indeed.

We stare at each other for longer than we probably should. Long enough that the steam rising from Sanzhar cools, and the ends of his hair frost in the cold.

"Your hair," I murmur, looping a strand that clings to his cheek around my fingers to show him. "It's frozen."

Eyes wide, Sanzhar glances at my hand, inches from his face. He bites his lip, then blurts out, "Bill!"

"What?" Witty conversationalist, I am not. At least not today. But Sanzhar ain't making a lick of sense.

"I'll talk to Bill!" His explanation rushes out as he runs his fingers across his mustache to smooth it down. "I'll step down from the project, so long as it goes to you."

Here, I thought we'd been having a moment, half-naked in an Alaskan hot spring, surrounded by snow-covered mountains, on the shortest day of the year. But it's the best time to talk about work, apparently.

I sigh, the disappointment bitter. If the moment is too much for Sanzhar, I am happy to talk about Bill. "You don't need to step down. There'll be other projects for me, and this will be good for you, to work with new people."

"Rory, you have the skills, the knowledge, the experience, the influence! And frankly, I don't have any of that yet, aside from the technical background. I never needed to wear so many hats in my old job, and I'm not ready for this. I'd rather learn on a smaller project." Sanzhar rubs his forehead. "I am so embarrassed that I didn't tell Bill off the second he said he was going to make me the project lead for your deal! I knew it wasn't fair, and I didn't—"

"Sanzhar, I get it!" I wrap my hand around his wrist, pulling his hand away from his stunning face to drag it back under the water, wishing I could see more of him. "Bill is hard to interrupt. He's the boss, and he don't take any hint of subordination well. If you're going to stand up to Bill for anything, please, tell him to stop calling you Sanny."

Sanzhar blinks at me, before a laugh bursts out of him. "Why the fuck does he call me Sanny? No one in my life has ever called me Sanny! At least call me Sandra No like my high school bullies did!"

I press my lips together, but I end up laughing with him. Underwater, his wrist slips through my fingers to take my hand. He steps closer, practically giggling against my neck. Every squeeze of his fingers intertwined with mine, each puff of warmth against my wet skin, the slow bat of his long eyelashes that are close enough to count—everything in this moment reminds me that I have not found a single opportunity to rub one out since I left for Alaska. The vibe in my bag has gone unused, even though my body and heart have both been screaming at me to make a move on Sanzhar, desperate for some relief. Even if I wanted to, I could not make myself step away from him. The distance would ache.

"Rory," Sanzhar sighs as our laughter dies down, his long hair now completely coated in rime from the cold, except at the roots and where his breath warms his mustache. "You keep that company afloat, and for what? To get ignored? Unsupported? Overlooked? He's so awful! To everyone, but especially to you." His hand tightens around mine. "You deserve so much better than Bill. We all do at that place, but you especially."

With a snort, I shake my head. "I'm used to it, honestly. It's my own fault for..." I trail off, shocked by the words that were about to escape from my psyche. Has being half-naked in a hot spring with Sanzhar really left me so vulnerable? Being trans doesn't mean I deserve any of this—the disrespect at work, the loneliness from my polycule rupturing, the isolation from my family. Why does my happiness in becoming myself warrant losing everything I care about? "It's not my fault," I murmur.

My partners are trying their best, but the awkwardness, the ache that has been plaguing us for months, it's not any of our faults. Not even mine, when I've been blaming myself for forcing my chosen family to stay close when they might have naturally drifted apart. I thought I was clinging to a sinking life raft, but they're all choosing me, too.

"Rory?" Sanzhar asks quietly, stepping closer.

"It's not my fault." My eyes are watering now. "Thank you for saying that, that I deserve better. Because I do. From Bill, from my family..." Blinking rapidly, I shake my head. "They need to fix their hearts, but I'm the one left hurting. And I don't deserve that, just because I'm trans."

Sanzhar slips his arms around my waist, pressing his lips to my shoulder. My chest bursts with warmth, because I know I didn't imagine that this time. "They're missing out, Rory, because you're wonderful."

I hug him back, arms spanning his broad shoulders, careful to avoid his frosted hair, so I don't break it. His skin is cool against mine under the steaming surface. The thin layer of mineral water trapped between us is the only thing keeping our bodies apart. He glances up at me, and my heart pounds in my throat.

"Rory," he murmurs. Glacially slow, one of his hands slips upward from my waist, burning a slow trail up my chest, my neck, my jaw. The other tightens around my hip, fingertips digging into the muscles just above my waistband.

I can't breathe, frozen in place, entranced by how even the eyelashes surrounding his wide brown eyes have frosted, fanning out into stark white at the tips. They stick together when he blinks, just like my lips do as his thumb brushes against them. His touch is featherlight, but this moment feels monumental. I swallow, leaning down—

"Starlight Lodge!" Alex yells from the other end of the pool. Sanzhar jumps away from me, and I can't help but feel guilty, though I don't know why. Sanzhar had to feel that, too! My chest tightens. Hadn't he? "This is your fifteen minute warning! Shower off and get changed into dry clothes, or else you're not getting in my van!"

"You want to shower first, or should I?" Sanzhar asks, his tone casual, bright. Am I delusional for thinking it sounds forced? Did that moment mean anything to him? With that closed off, polite smile on his face, Sanzhar's expression becomes unreadable. Maybe that's my answer. The subtle rejection makes my stomach churn in disappointment and embarrassment. How many times does this guy have to tell me he's not interested?

"Go ahead," I mutter, forcing a casual smile of my own. "Want me to get your towel, freeze baby?"

His smile goes crooked as Sanzhar chuckles. "I thought that was a given."

I can't help but grin back. It's a relief to see the real Sanzhar, the friend I've made, emerge again from behind his polite facade. I haven't ruined this by projecting my growing feelings where they don't exist. Getting over a crush is easy; I've done it many times. But I don't think I could handle the loss of our friendship, not when Sanzhar seems as lonely as I do.

Chapter Eleven

When did I turn into such a simp? There is no logical reason why I am shivering in the locker room, instead of showering. No one else is in here yet, except us and Alex, who sings from a shower stall across the room. It's safe enough for me to rinse off the minerals from the hot spring with Sanzhar.

In a different stall of course.

Unless...

No. Sanzhar ran into the shower without a change of clothes, and I have the locker key. Out of my ingrained sense of decency—and because, despite all signs to give up, this crush is relentless, so I'll bend over backwards for his praise—I remain standing there, waiting. Dripping onto the tile floor, my body violently shakes from the cold as I try to shove the key in the hole. The least I can do is set his clothes next to the shower for him.

Once my phone is powered back up, there are a few notifications. A missed call from Bill, which is weird; he left a voicemail, which is even weirder. With a scoff of annoyance, I check my texts instead. I don't really want to hear what he has to say.

In the polycule group chat, there are some solstice greetings, all directed at me instead of all of us. Presumably because I'm doing something to mark the occasion, but it does not help me feel less like a child of newly divorced parents. But, as Sanzhar so recently reminded me, it's not my fault. They decided to break up with each other, and not me. Both couples decided together to remain friends and keep up our big group chat, instead of starting two smaller ones. While I appreciate that, I have to trust that they chose that because it's what *they* want too, not simply for my sake.

There's another text from Gina, asking if I told Bill I was taking PTO last minute. I frown. I had sent an email before I left the office on Friday, letting him know I was taking a couple of days off this week. Since half the office and all of our clients would be off, I didn't think I'd needed more planning than that. Nothing will be so urgent that I can't handle it on Wednesday. Besides, Bill is on PTO this week, and it's already after one in the afternoon here, which means it's the end of the workday in Minneapolis. I don't understand what is so urgent that my PTO is causing issues.

As I'm frowning at my phone, another text from Gina pops up. This one just tells me that she'll try and calm Bill down.

My heart leaps to my throat. Calm him down? What the hell is he upset about? That I took two days off, during our slowest week of the year?

Setting Sanzhar's clothes on the bench inside the changing vestibule, I play the voicemail. My ears are roaring so loud, I wonder if I'll need to turn the volume up. I can't even register Alex's singing anymore.

But Bill's booming voice is as inescapable as ever, and I flinch at the dark edge in his normally boisterous tone. "When the cat's away, the mice will play, huh, Rory? I should have expected you'd be a sneaking rat the second you didn't get your way. Did you think I wouldn't notice you were missing? I'm not someone you want to test, Rory. If your ass is not in your seat tomorrow, you're fired."

My hands shake as I hang up the phone, now more from adrenaline than the cold. I can't afford to lose this job. I love the work, even if I can't stand Bill. I *need* this job, because what are my alternatives if I lose it? Trying to find an opening in tech as a trans guy, in a state where I am physically and legally safe, where I can afford rent, in this economy? That's impossible. Everything is tense enough with my fractured polycule already; asking to stay with Dawn and Sarah over Ducky and Charlie, or vice versa, might break it entirely.

"You okay?" Sanzhar asks, making me freeze as blind panic sets in. He's got the towel wrapped around his hair, already in his long johns and olive green wool sweater. The hem hangs down his thick thighs. "You look flushed. You didn't get hypothermia waiting for me out here, did you?" He presses his hand to the back of my forehead.

I step back, chucking my phone in the locker to grab my clothes. "I'm fine."

"Rory?" He puts his hand on my arm. "What's wrong? You're shaking."

"I'm fine!" I force a smile. "Just cold. It's freezing."

It's not Sanzhar's fault that the life I've built for myself—the life that's brought me so much joy because it's *mine*, on my own terms—is teetering on the verge of destruction because Bill is on a power trip.

I just wanted a break.

Pushing past Sanzhar, I yank the shower curtain behind me, and finally let my feelings rush to the surface. Tears roll down my cheeks as I turn the water on.

A hot shower will help me figure out what to do. Even if it means leaving early, missing my chance to see the aurora, missing my last night with Sanzhar… I swallow a silent sob as I step into the scalding spray. I have to get myself under control, remember what's truly important. This is just a vacation, an escape. My life takes priority, and I have to save it.

Chapter Twelve

Just as we're piling out of the van back at the Starlight Lodge, my phone rings. I'm relieved to see it's Gina calling, instead of Bill. The whole ride back, Sanzhar was too sweet, too concerned for me, and the upheaval was too fresh, too raw to tell him about Bill's message. I don't trust myself to stay composed with all of these strangers around, and I still don't have a plan formed yet. So I pretended to nod off the whole way back as my mind raced.

If there's one thing I'm good at, it's keeping my head in a crisis. Middle child gumption taught me how to push through my feelings, how to win people over by learning what makes them tick. Keeping my job was the easy part to figure out; I can catch an Uber and book the earliest flight out, then spend the next few weeks kissing Bill's ass 'til this all washes out. Show him I've not gotten too big for my britches. I've let my own arrogance, my lack of respect for Bill, change how I act around him. I've forgotten that I need his support more than he needs mine.

The part of this plan I can't figure out is how to tell Sanzhar. How to accept the cost of leaving, how to sacrifice my own selfish wants because Bill is forcing my hand.

"Hey G, hold on a minute." Forcing a smile at Sanzhar, I gesture to my phone. "I gotta take this. You want to check with Gladys on that early dinner, and I'll meet you back at the dome?"

Holding the door to the lodge open for me, Sanzhar narrows his eyes. "You sure you're okay?"

"Stop worrying, Tursyn! I'm just tuckered out." I snort, trying to hide how exposed he makes me feel. He'll be upset that I have to leave, and I don't want to hurt him, not yet. Maybe he'll understand. Maybe he won't take it personally. "That's what I get for keeping us up all night, right?" Pressing the phone to my ear, I practically run down the canvas hallway towards our dome. "Apologies Gina, I'm here."

"I'm sorry, 'Tursyn'? Was that *Sanzhar* you were just talking to?" she shrieks. "What exactly were you doing keeping *him* awake all night? Aren't you in Alaska?"

Heat rushes to my face as I shut the trapdoor behind me, leaving it unlocked for Sanzhar. "It's not what it sounded like!"

"Rory, you're taking a secret, last-minute vacation to some remote wilderness, with *Sanzhar*, and making jokes about keeping him up all night?" Gina tsks through the phone. "I don't know what other explanation there could possibly be."

"It don't matter, G!" I groan, stomping to the bathroom to grab my toiletry bag. On my way back, I stop at the woodstove to toss a few logs in and bank the coals. At least that will keep Sanzhar warm tonight, after I'm gone. Wedging the phone between my shoulder and my ear, I take a moment to fuss with the air intake to be sure he doesn't freeze. "Did you talk to Bill? Is he really gonna fire me? What even happened that anyone noticed I was gone?"

"That's the thing! Nothing! He asked me to periodically check to make sure folks were online while he's gone. You're on PTO according to the timecard portal, so I don't understand why he's pissed when I listed you as out of office. You're allowed to take time off." Gina sighs in a way that tells me the situation is hopeless, and my heart sinks. "He's just looking for an excuse to be a controlling dick because he knows you're upset about the Aurora Labs project."

"It doesn't matter *why* he's doing it, Gina!" I snap—unfairly, because Gina is in no position to do anything about it, not without putting her own job at risk. I huff as I toss my duffel bag onto the bed to pack, trying to get a hold of the anger exploding in my chest. The ache of disappointment is already building in my throat. "The fact of the matter is Bill is going to fire me unless I fly back home within the next few hours, so I have to go—"

"What?"

I whirl around to find Sanzhar halfway through the trapdoor, his expression frozen into a tense mask. I shake my head at him to... I don't even know what I'm asking him for. To stay quiet until I hang up with Gina? To not get upset with me for bailing like this? To not ask questions so I don't have to talk about it?

Brow furrowing, Sanzhar doesn't listen to any of my silent pleas. "Bill can't fire you."

"He can!" I huff. "He will."

"This must be some misunderstanding!" Sanzhar shakes his head, kicking the trapdoor shut with a slam. "Bill isn't *that* stupid."

In my ear, Gina lets out a sardonic laugh.

"Gina, I gotta go. Text me any updates, please. Thank you! You're the best!" I hang up before she can respond, and start shoving my clothes into my bag, even my still-damp, ice-cold trunks. "It's not a misunderstanding. I didn't exactly ask permission to take PTO. I just did it, figuring no one would care." I huff against the tears forming in my eyes. How foolish I'd been, to think Bill would understand. I should have known better.

"Rory," Sanzhar's voice softens, which makes me feel worse, somehow. I'd rather he be upset than pity me. "You taking a couple days off during the holidays is barely an inconvenience, let alone something worth firing anyone for! Let me talk some sense into Bill."

"Don't!" I snap, shoving my pajamas in my bag. "I'll just catch a flight home, and kiss Bill's ass until this all washes out. I've got it under control."

"No." Sanzhar yanks my pajamas out of my bag and tosses them on the floor, eyes blazing behind his glasses. My heart aches at the hurt on his face. "We have a plan, Rory. It's our last night here! We're going to ruin our sleep schedules, and stay up all night, and watch the fucking northern lights together!"

"Sanzhar!" I shake out my pajamas to shove them back in my bag, but he's already pulling everything else out of my duffel. My swim trunks land with a wet plop on the threadbare carpet, and my toiletries spill out across the duvet, including the bullet vibe which has gone unused. I barely notice, shoving everything back into the zippered pouch. "I don't want to, but I have to go! I can't lose my job!"

"We can fix this, Rory!" Sanzhar sits on my duffel bag, fishing his phone out of his coat pocket. "Let me try, at least! I can call Bill—"

"Look, you got no dog in this fight. You don't need to fix nothing!" I try to tug my duffel out from under him, gently pulling him off of the bed. Before I can blink, I'm lying faceup on top of my bag, wondering what the hell just happened.

Covering my mouth with his hand, Sanzhar straddles my chest. "I'm going to try, at least. If I can't get through to him, then you can go. But I want you to stay here. With me." Though his eyes are bright with anger, Sanzhar looks as collected as usual. There's that same spark of determination in his upright posture, as there was when he matter-of-factly informed me of our plans this morning.

Hand still pressed over my mouth, Sanzhar is already calling Bill before I can stop him. I can only lay there helplessly, my back arched over my duffel bag half filled with clothes. "Hi Bill— Yes, happy holiday—" While I can't make out what Bill's saying, his voice sounds much happier than the message he left for me. Part of me hopes that Sanzhar was right, that maybe this was all a misunderstanding. "Glad to hear— Bill, I hate to call on your vac—" Sanzhar rolls his eyes, then practically shouts. "You need to give the Aurora Labs project to Rory. I'm not the right person to lead it, so I'm going to step back from the deal."

The line goes quiet for a long moment, then Bill explodes. I can't make out most of it, but the snatches of vitriol I do hear—some directed at me, some at Sanzhar—make tears roll down my temples as I stare skyward. The cloudless sky is orange with the setting sun, hazy and thick. Sanzhar sits silently, hand still pressed to my mouth. Eyebrows raised, his lips are pressed into a thin line as Bill rants on and on.

When Bill finally tires himself out, Sanzhar clears his throat. "Well, I was going to give you my two weeks' notice if you didn't reassign the project to Rory." I try to sit up, but my protests are muffled by Sanzhar's hand. He pushes me back down onto the bed with a scowl. "But after that tirade, I am quitting, effective immediately. I'll return my laptop and any other company property to Gina on Wednesday. Thank you for all of the opportunities you've provided me, and for the clarity from this conversation. Enjoy your holidays, Bill, and go fuck yourself." Before he hangs up, Sanzhar yells into the microphone, "Oh, and my name is *not* Sanny, it's Sanzhar! It's not hard to say, you racist piece of shit!"

When he hangs up on the shouting Bill, Sanzhar doesn't take his hand from my mouth, but he does let me sit up. He shuffles down my hips to settle on my lap, barely offering me an unreadable glance when my hands find his thighs.

"Why the hell would you do that?" I ask from behind his hand.

Hitting "call" on another contact, Sanzhar levels a look at me, as if the answer should be obvious. "Hi Emmy! Happy Solstice! How are you?" His voice is night and day from the last phone call, bright and chipper and genuine. "I'm not interrupting you, am I?"

Sanzhar beams as the other person on the line cheerfully greets him, as if he hadn't just listened to five minutes of bigoted ranting from our boss. "That's part of the reason I'm calling, yeah, to see if you still have an opening for me?" He blushes as the other person audibly squeals through the phone.

Jealousy burns hot, tempered by admiration for how bold Sanzhar has become. I wish finding a new job for me was as easy as calling up an old friend.

"Aw, I've missed working with you too! Do you by any chance have room for a second engineer? You know I wouldn't ask for just anyone, he is someone you do *not* want to pass on."

My cheeks burn as Sanzhar smiles at me. Oh my stars, is finding me a new job just as easy as calling an old friend?

"Oh, and an admin position? I'm stealing everyone with talent from Bill. I'll text you their contact info, but the engineer is Rory Callahan, and the admin is Gina Cortez."

My eyes fill once again, and I whimper pitifully behind Sanzhar's hand. Of course, he thought of Gina. No one has ever stood up for me like this. Never put me first, never put their necks out for me like this. Not only has he quit his job in solidarity, but Sanzhar is working to find me a new one without being asked? And looking out for my work wife, too? My heart pounds in my chest, and I squeeze his thighs that are spread over mine. It's frustrating how—even if he was letting me talk right now—nothing I could say would ever be enough to show how profoundly grateful and touched I am in this moment.

"Oh, and one more thing," Sanzhar murmurs, his tone turning secretive. "Could you find a way where Rory and I are not on the same team? Or like, at least not reporting to the same person in the org chart? He might be a good fit as a team lead, to be a liaison between the dev and sales teams, or maybe a consultant in product? He's a real jack of all trades." His cheeks go red as the other person singsongs something I can't catch, and he looks up at the sky. "Look, Em, I don't want to get into it right now, but yeah, I am sitting on his lap as I'm talking to you, if that answers your question."

"Oh?" I smile, the sound muffled by his palm as the other person teases him more.

Sanzhar groans in embarrassment; my heart feels like it might burst out of my chest. "Yeah, yeah, yeah, I know. Like I said, I don't really want to talk about it right now, when he can literally hear every word I'm saying." Sanzhar must feel how hard I'm beaming against his palm, but he refuses to look at me. "Yes, absolutely, we should get coffee soon. Okay, text me when you know more— Thank you, as always, for everything— Love you too, Em! Bye! Bye, I'm hanging up now!"

As soon as he's off the phone, Sanzhar finally pulls his hand away from my mouth with an embarrassed smile. His eyes meet mine, just as the sky dims around us when the sun sets over the mountains. "Why don't Minnesotans know how to end a damn phone—"

I interrupt Sanzhar with my lips against his.

Chapter Thirteen

Sanzhar's sharp intake of breath when I kiss him is the most glorious sound I've ever heard, made all the sweeter by his fist twisting my sweatshirt to pull me closer, and the "finally," he murmurs against my lips.

That is all I need to show him exactly how much I appreciate him, how much I want him—*been* wanting him, since I woke up with him surrounding me the other morning. My hands tighten around his thighs to tug him closer as he deepens the kiss, tongue delving between my lips with a satisfied huff through his nose.

Kissing Sanzhar is better than I ever imagined in any of my fantasies over the past couple of days. When he slept wrapped around me last night, his parted lips were mere inches from mine; I'd imagined him waking up and leaning in to kiss me softly, sweetly.

There is nothing soft or sweet about this.

The energy between us is urgent and needy and desperate. Sanzhar is kneeling above me. His fist in my hair tilts my head back so far that it almost hurts to breathe, and his mustache is rough against my upper lip. His cock against my stomach is hard—incredibly validating after waking up with his knee pressed against my aching, needy dick two mornings in a row.

When I suck Sanzhar's lower lip between my teeth and gently bite down, his thighs tremble under my hands with a breathy curse. I slide my hand from his thighs to his hips, encircling him to roll him onto his back, moving us up the bed far enough to straddle him. We groan together as I grind against his cock.

It's everything I can do not to rut against him desperately, but I let him set the pace, matching each slow roll of his hips as he arches up into me. Brown eyes heavy with lust, Sanzhar blinks ever so slowly. His tongue wets his lips when he whispers my name. Bending down, I kiss him again, softer now, sweeter, though my hands are fists gripping his chest as I fight for some semblance of self-control.

"Rory," Sanzhar groans, his hand dragging slowly up my back to fist my hair.

I love the tug that follows, groaning with the sparks that tight yank sends down my spine.

Until I realize he's pulling me away.

"Hold on a sec," he pants.

"Oh my stars, I am so sorry!" Stomach dropping like snow's been slipped down my back, I spring off of him, scrambling to the foot of the bed, horrified at myself. He just put his neck on the line for me, and I took that as consent to maul him? My chest tightens in panic. "I should have asked!"

"Rory..." Sanzhar sits up with a groan. "You do not need to apologize."

"You're ace!" My hands ball into fists as I wave them helplessly in the air. "I mean, I should have asked anyway, but *especially* because you're ace!"

"If I didn't like it, I would have stopped you much, much sooner. Trust me, I was an enthusiastic participant in *all* of that." When I don't stop fretting, Sanzhar leans forward to grab my wrist, pulling me closer to sit next to him on the bed. "Come back here."

I obey, if only to look him in the eyes, so he can see I mean what I'm saying. I fix the glasses I've knocked crooked in my enthusiasm as I cup his face, and smooth his mustache with my thumbs. "I promise, I have nothing but the utmost respect for you, and I value our friendship, and I never want to do anything to compromise that! Nothing like that will ever happen again! I swear!"

"Rory," Sanzhar murmurs. "Don't make promises I don't want you to keep."

Confusion twists my mouth into a frown. "What?"

"Callahan, I don't know how much clearer I can be." Sanzhar frowns back. "Shut up and kiss me."

"But you said— What about— Yeah, no, okay. Got it." I shut up and kiss him, devouring his mouth, unsure if we're picking up where we left off because I still don't know why he told me to wait. My hands tangle in his hair as he pushes me onto my back. The soft strands, still damp from the shower after the hot springs, catch between my fingers.

"Is this okay?" he asks, his voice husky in my ear as he grinds against me. Even through our many layers, his cock is hard against my thigh.

"Fuck yes," I hiss, wrapping a leg around his hip to angle us so that he's pressing against the seam of my jeans. The friction sends me climbing skyward. "Is this okay for you? I don't want to make you uncomfortable."

"For someone so intelligent..." His lips find a spot on my throat that makes me whimper. "And curious." His teeth scrape against my skin, and I groan, rolling my hips to chase the pleasure. From his trembling breath, he's enjoying it, too, even if he hasn't directly answered my question. "And understanding—"

"I don't like where this is going," I huff with a smile, arching my back to give him more room.

Sanzhar groans against my neck. "It's about to get worse, because I just remembered we have to stop."

"We do?" To my disappointment, Sanzhar pulls back, looming over me. His hair is a curtain, blocking the fading light around us. The absence of his thigh leaves the gap between mine painfully empty.

"I cannot possibly comprehend how you, of all people, did not think to ask me a single question about my aroace experience." Lips swollen, Sanzhar smiles as he cups my jaw. "You remember when you said you were polyamorous, and I was like, 'oh, what does that mean for you?' You can ask those kinds of questions too, you know? Arguably, you *should* ask those questions, given we've been dancing around whatever is happening between us for the better part of the weekend."

"Oh. Uh..." Sanzhar smirks down at me expectantly, while I sputter. My mind can only form pleas for him to touch me, but that's not what he wants to hear right now. "Wh- What does that mean for you?"

"Great question, Callahan." Sanzhar pats my cheek. "For me, I am indifferent to sex and relationships. I don't crave it, but with the right person, I enjoy dating and physical intimacy in most forms, especially someone I'm comfortable with."

My mouth hangs open as my mind races to process this new information. "Most forms?" I hold back the "show me" that threatens to spill out.

Sanzhar winces, and I worry my private thoughts have somehow crossed a line. "Not to be crass, but I don't really like sticking my junk in a hole, or vice versa." My surprise comes out as a strangled yip; that is not what I expected him to say. "Sure, it feels good, but hands are better, and I'd rather suck someone off than have them fuck me. Less clean up."

"Oh." Apparently, I have not crossed a line. I am nowhere *near* the line. My whole body buzzes at the idea of Sanzhar on his knees, his hair wrapped in my fist while he sucks me off. I exhale, trying not to get ahead of myself by thinking with my dick, when he wants to have a reasoned conversation. "So if you were on Grindr, you'd be a side?"

He nods. "Yeah, mine says side looking for friends with potential benefits."

That strangled yip flies out again. "Wait, you actually have one?"

"Aroace people can be on Grindr too." Sanzhar snorts. "If I'm feeling particularly lonely or touch starved, I prefer being with queer people—men usually. Just, affectionate quality time with someone I can talk to. You know the relationship staircase, where most couples date, then become exclusive, then move in together, get engaged, et cetera?" I nod. The polycule made a whole color coded diagram when talks of marriage between Sarah and Dawn first came up. "Well, I stop at casual dating, or perhaps a situationship, some might call it. I'm not opposed to exclusivity, but more often than not, the people who pressure me into becoming exclusive then pressure me to move in together, and I like my space." He shrugs, but I resonate with the undercurrent of pain in the way his eyes flick away from me.

On the diagram my partners and I made, Dawn and Sarah went to the top, marriage and kids and sharing everything together. Ducky and Charlie went half that far, all the way up to cohabitating, though not to the point of blending financials or committing to anything legal. I stayed near the bottom, where Sanzhar is, in the blurry area between casual dating and exclusivity. Part of the reason I moved out of the house we all used to share; I love them all, but I need a space of my own. Except where Sanzhar calls it a situationship, I call it commitment, love, family—just not in the way most of the world defines those words.

"Not that there aren't cis women who only want to be casual, but the expectations are different." Sanzhar shrugs again, forcing a casual air I don't buy for a second. "Both in relationships and sex and gender expectations. In my experience, they tend to take it personally when I don't want to fuck them or meet their families. Queer guys are generally more open to what I have to offer."

"There's no heterosexual equivalent of being a side," I chuckle. "I am too, by the way. A side, I mean. With cis guys, anyway." I decide he don't need to hear the specific effects T has had on my front hole. Or about how I enjoy topping my partners. But those are *their* straps, not mine, even if I wear them. They are definitely not for me to use with anyone else I hook up with.

Sanzhar smirks down at me, then softens with a bite of his lower lip. "I guess, this is all a very long way to say that I like you, Rory. Immensely. And I'm really looking forward to getting to know you better, in every way that works for us."

"Oh?" My face warms. "You mean professionally, right?"

Fingers tightening around my jaw, Sanzhar practically growls in frustration. I lose the fight against my grin. When he realizes I'm teasing, his groan turns into an exasperated laugh. "I can't stand you."

"No, you like me. Immensely," I tease, then blurt out, "I'd like that. Getting to know you real well, in whatever ways work for us. Dating. Quality time. Because I like you too. Maybe a little more than immensely." I rise up on my elbows. "I don't want the staircase neither, so I can't imagine I'd ever pressure you into more than you want. And I'm not just saying that because I'm a people pleaser."

He snorts. "Oh, well, that's a promising start."

I reach for him to kiss him again, but Sanzhar pushes me back down with an affectionate smile. At the firm press of his hand against my chest, I melt into a helpless puddle.

"However, I didn't stop us to have this overdue conversation," he continues. "I stopped us because we have a very excellent plan in motion to stay awake all night. That is...if you still want that." Sanzhar's eyes flick away. "If you want to leave, to keep your job, I understand. I just...I wanted to give you an option, a choice! So that you could stay, if you wanted. Especially now that I won't be there, Bill has to know he needs you. Yes, finding a job is harder for you, but I can't stand the thought of you staying there because fucking *Bill* is your best option. And I can't promise this will work out—"

"Tursyn, I'm not going anywhere," I interrupt Sanzhar's rambling. "You have no idea how much I appreciate you sticking your neck out for me. Even if your old job can't hire me, I do deserve better than that place. No, I'm staying here tonight, with you, and Bill can choke."

"Oh good!" Sanzhar beams. "Because Gladys is probably wondering where the hell we are, and she promised me an extra piece of garlic bread."

With pitiful whine, I blink up at him. "Really? Dinner? Now?" I huff, annoyed at myself for already pressuring him into making out with me more, when he just said he wants to eat. "No, my apologies. You're right."

"Hey," Sanzhar murmurs, leaning down over me. His hair brushes my cheek as it falls over his face, and his hand slides up my chest to cup my jaw. "That doesn't mean I don't want to stay here, that I don't want to kiss you senseless. But I am determined that *if* there's an aurora tonight, we're going to experience it together. And that means we are going to eat our early ass dinner and get some rest, so we can stay awake after Therèse leaves for the night." Sanzhar brushes his lips against mine, so gently I can't help but gasp. "We have all night, all right?"

I nod, a little embarrassed by his reassurance, but feeling more seen than anything. Most people overlook me, or take me for granted, the way my family did my whole life until I made them see the real me. My partners understand just how fragile I can be, under my layers of good manners and lighthearted jokes. But this whole weekend, Sanzhar saw through my fake smiles and attempts at humor. Every time, he has said exactly what I needed to hear to feel a little more secure, a little more safe with him.

I grin, finding that easy humor that has become second nature. A real smile to let him know that he's safe with me, too. That I won't demand more than he wants to give. "Considering we're both unemployed now, we've got all the time in the world."

Chapter Fourteen

Sanzhar's plan overlooked one key flaw: I can't sleep worth a damn.

I've closed my eyes, drifted off a time or two as twilight deepened into full dark, but true rest has been impossible. How could I possibly sleep when every nerve in my body is buzzing? How could I relax when Sanzhar is, as usual, wrapped around me, nestled so closely that he might as well be a second blanket? Only now, there's nothing holding back my delight in being so close with him. No guilt for wanting him, no constant reminders to stop crushing on him.

No, I haven't been able to relax since the hot spring, since Sanzhar stuck his neck out for me, since our kiss. Especially after he texted me a goddamned screenshot of his latest STI test casually over dinner. While Gladys ladled mulled wine into a thermos for us to share tonight, I politely listened to everything she had to say about her knee replacement. Only to choke on my own spit in surprise at what he texted me. Sanzhar's little smirk as Therèse handed me some water made me buzz with anticipation, eager to get back to our dome.

Only for his sadistic ass to insist we actually sleep.

He's sprawled over my side as I lie on my back, staring up at the stars. The broad shoulders and thick torso weighing me down are comforting, the head tucked under my chin and hair brushing my neck endearing. While his breath is deep and even, he's not asleep either; instead, Sanzhar absentmindedly traces my chest and stomach beneath my shirt. His hand sears a slow path along the scars, the hair sprouting across my chest, down to my waistband, and back up, over and over and over. More sensual than sexual, his touch leaves me craving more.

I'm no less affectionate, palm pressed against his back, memorizing how the muscles of his shoulder blade move under his skin. My other hand strokes the lines of his waist and hip, his warm skin soft and supple under the blankets. I had never considered myself touch starved, but after this weekend, the idea of sleeping without Sanzhar's thigh between mine, without his contented huffs against my neck when he settles in, makes my chest ache.

"What does a relationship look like to you?" I ask, giving up the pretense of sleeping. It must be after midnight, when Therèse was scheduled to leave, but we didn't set an alarm—as if we knew we wouldn't get much rest.

Wiggling against me to settle in deeper, Sanzhar lets out one of those endearing, contented huffs before answering. "What do you mean?"

"Do you want to stay over at my place sometimes, or me at yours? Do we go out to do coupley things together, or stay in?" I shrug the shoulder he's not laying on. "We're in kind of a weird place, getting together on vacation instead of real life. What do you want? Long-term, short-term. What happens when we're BAU?"

Sanzhar snorts, and I thrill at how his smile feels against my collarbone. "Did you just call our lives 'business as usual'?"

"Well, I reckon we might still be testing, given that we're both going back without jobs," I tease. "We're not quite to the deployment stage, at least until we're employed. So what does the SIT phase look like for December Rory and Sanzhar Sprint One?"

"Maybe this was a mistake," Sanzhar laughs. "I did not sign up for bad tech metaphors."

"What kind of bad metaphors would you like me to use?" I squeeze him tight, threatening to tickle him again. "Fair warning, they're all nerdy."

Sanzhar grabs my hand before I can reach any sensitive spots, lacing our fingers together in a firm grip. He brings my hand to his lips so he can press a quick kiss against my knuckles. "Long-term, my ideal relationship is one of mutual support where we rely on each other. Emergency contacts, keys to each other's places, bring each other soup when we're sick, that sort of thing. Emotional trust, I suppose, where we know each other in ways that I don't often reach with other people." He shrugs in my arms, and I squeeze his hand; I've learned on this trip that Sanzhar doesn't shrug unless he's pretending to be nonchalant about something deeply personal. "But that's a lot to ask when we're just getting started. Short-term? Simply companionship. So yes, hanging out, staying the night sometimes, going on dates. I'm not fussy how often or where. I will admit, I am a homebody, but I have been..." he pauses, his fingers tightening around my waist. "Lonely, lately."

I shift ever so slightly, just enough to kiss his temple. "Me too," I say against his hair. "Want to talk about it?"

He sighs. "I dunno. I'm fine being alone most of the time. Like I said, my mom is the same way, so I'm used to it. But I'm about to turn thirty next year, and I'm realizing the most fun I had in my twenties was with other people. I want more friends, I want more adventures with them, I want to be seen by people."

"I see you," I murmur.

Sanzhar looks up at me with his crooked smile. "I'm surprised to hear you've been feeling lonely, when you have so many partners."

"What do you know, polyamorous people can be lonely too!" I snort. "Normally, it's not so bad, but this time of year gets hard. Traditions and quality time were always a big deal for my family, so the holidays were like, our thing." My chest tightens, remembering all of the silly rituals my family had. This year, there will be no cinnamon rolls in the morning, no contest to see who can do the worst wrapping job, no drunken carols after the brandy-to-eggnog ratio gets out of hand. "I hope they at least think of me, wonder how I'm doing, maybe feel a little guilty about cutting me off. But my nieces are just small kids. They'll never know me, and that shit sucks. It goes against every value they taught me to cut me off like this, and it's not fair."

"You're right, it's not." Sanzhar brushes a tear from my cheek that I hadn't known had fallen, his expression soft.

"My apologies, didn't mean to get all emotional." I wipe my face on my shoulder, hoping I can keep the waterworks under control for once. "My partners don't really get it. Sarah, the one who just got married, kind of does because her parents don't support her either, but she's basically been adopted by her new in-laws. And the other two are doing the holidays with Ducky's family, right down the block from my parents. I know they feel bad that I'll be by myself, but I'd feel worse tagging along and pretending to be their friend, when they're introducing Charlie to Mama Duck. Of the three of us, she was the only one of our parents who let us be us, growing up."

"None of their families know about your relationship?" he asks. "Even now?"

I shake my head. "Maybe one day, but no, none of us are publicly out as polyamorous. Sarah and Ducky were nesting partners back before we all moved to Minnesota, so I've always been the strangely-close friend. It's funny, how we're all fiercely proud of being queer and gender nonconforming, that polyamory is the one part of our lives we keep secret, even though I'm sure Mama Duck wouldn't care. Our friends in Minnesota know, of course, but I haven't even told Gina. I think you're the only person I've told who doesn't know my other partners."

"I'm honored," Sanzhar kisses my cheek. "So where do I fit into *your* life? What do you want out of," he scoffs, "December Rory and Sanzhar Sprint One? We need a better naming convention for this."

I chuckle at his endearing annoyance. "Same as you, I reckon."

Sanzhar levels a look at me. "That sounds rather people pleaser of you, Callahan."

"I swear it's true!" I smile, running a hand up and down his back. "I just want someone who wants me around, without feeling like I'm a burden or inconvenience."

Silence is Sanzhar's only response.

I rush to fill it. "So yeah, companionship, I suppose. Long-term... I guess feeling like a priority? As long as I'm not getting in the way of the rest of your life, I mean."

"Is that how your polycule is making you feel? Like you're an inconvenience, or a burden?" Sanzhar asks quietly.

"Not intentionally," I huff. "Shit's just awkward right now, and I don't want to rock the boat when it's already listing."

"I know I'm not one to talk," Sanzhar says, turning onto his stomach. His thigh slips across my hip until he's practically straddling me. "Given that I'm no expert at relationships, and I avoid conflict like the plague. But perhaps some honesty will help right it. If your partners care about you as much as you say, they would want to know how you're feeling."

"Maybe," I admit, my hands finding Sanzhar's hips as if a magnet draws them there.

"No, Callahan, *definitely*." Sanzhar's smile is soft as he leans in, pressing his forehead to mine. "Not feeling like a burden is less than the bare minimum, and I'm sure your partners would agree with me that you deserve so much more. If you're ever feeling like an inconvenience to me, I want you to tell me right away, so we can fix that together."

I snort. "Tursyn, in the past forty-eight hours, I've crashed your vacation and lost you your job. That's the definition of a burden."

Sanzhar sits up on his elbow with a frustrated groan. "Rory, you cannot seriously believe that I am in any way bothered by any of that. Do you know how excited I was when I saw you in the lobby? Finally, I thought, here's my chance to get to know this interesting, intelligent, competent man, who I have wanted to be friends with since I started. I was so fucking relieved that maybe I'd get to experience all of this," he gestures around the starry dome surrounding us, "with someone. With *you*!"

My heart pounds as he leans in close again, kissing my forehead so softly my insides melt. My eyes water, and my tongue sticks to the roof of my mouth. Fuck, I'm gonna cry again, aren't I?

"Rory, you gave me a reason to stand up for myself. To grow a fucking spine and do what I've known I needed to for months." Sanzhar's brown eyes are wide as he looks at me earnestly. "I haven't been happy, and the whole time, I thought *I* was the problem. But no, both of us, we deserve better than that place, and we're going to find it, together. Okay?"

As always with Sanzhar, I'm incapable of finding the right words. For anyone else, I might have strung together some heartfelt explanation for just how deeply his words touched me, probably blubbering the whole time. I'll work on it, because Sanzhar deserves everything and more. But for now, I simply kiss him. Soft and sweet, so he knows that this kiss is one of appreciation, not lust.

Sanzhar exhales softly, melting against me to deepen the kiss.

So much for sweet; the moan that escapes me is pure sin, pent up over days of unquenched longing. My fingers bury into that soft hair at the back of his head, slotting our mouths together. His lips part around my name, and his tongue caresses mine.

Before I can think to ask what he wants, Sanzhar is tugging at my T-shirt, pulling it roughly over my head. "You're so fucking hot," he murmurs, cool hands running down my chest and stomach. I preen under his appreciative gaze, puffing out my chest to make my abs more defined (a pose I unabashedly practice in the mirror, because why wouldn't I admire the body that finally looks like me?). "I can't believe you've been hiding all this under those dorky shirts you wear."

"My shirts aren't dorky." I wrinkle my nose.

"I have yet to see you wear any shirt without Pokémon, Star Wars, or Jojo's Bizarre Adventure on it." Sanzhar nods to where my T-shirt is sprawled on the foot of the bed, leaving Psyduck's vacant expression staring at the sky. His teasing smirk erases any comeback about his nerd-chic sweaters and bow ties at work. "Just take the compliment, Rory. You're hot. And I say this as someone who has spent a lot of time wondering what the big deal is about naked bodies, so I'm not blowing smoke up your ass."

"Fine, compliment accepted. I would *return* the compliment, but I haven't seen you yet," I tease, tugging the hem of his sweatshirt. "You were like the Flash running to and from the showers earlier."

Sanzhar laughs. "I get cold easily."

"I'll keep you warm," I murmur, sitting up to kiss his neck, slipping my hand under the fabric to stroke his soft skin. On our last night here, I've finally gotten the hang of the woodstove; the dome is almost too warm for me, so hopefully it's good enough for Sanzhar. "Let me see you."

With a bashful smile, Sanzhar pulls his sweatshirt and tee off, exposing the thick torso and broad shoulders that have made me feel safe, cared for, and painfully horny the past couple of nights. His body looks as glorious as it feels, dark nipples tempting against his light brown skin. A trail of tantalizing hair disappears under the elastic of his lounge pants. His cock is half-hard already, bulging at the flannel.

I'm tempted, but I touch his sides instead, running my hand up to tug him back down into a kiss. "Glorious, every inch of you. Inside and out."

Sanzhar's ears and nose turn pink before he kisses me, our bodies slotting together like they have every time we sleep. The difference now is the charged energy in how we move together, his cock hardening against my hip, the squeak when my thumb brushes his nipple.

"Was that a good sound?" I ask, grinning as he answers by shoving his chest in my face. I lap at him at first, then suck the hardening nipple, nibbling gently until his hips jerk and his fingers tighten in my hair. Gripping his ass with one hand, I slide the other around to the front, glancing up at him for permission.

He nods, brows furrowed and lips parted. His brown eyes squeeze shut as I tug his loungers down, licking my fingers before wrapping them around the thick cock that springs out. Sucking his puffy lower lip between his teeth, Sanzhar's breath turns ragged with each slow stroke of my hand, each lap of my tongue against his chest, each squeeze of the firm, juicy ass he's been hiding in khakis this whole time.

But before I get to see how he looks when he comes, he stops me with a pained groan. "I don't want to come too soon."

"Why not?" I pout, allowing him to pull my hand away.

"Because I know myself, and I will fall asleep." His loungers are gone by the time he wiggles under the blankets with me to press kisses up my chest and neck. "And I want to get you off before that happens." His hand slips around to the front of my boxers, pressing gently against my dick.

With a loud moan, I involuntarily arch, trapping his hand between my thighs to rut against the tentative touch.

"Can you show me how you like it?" Sanzhar asks, eyebrows furrowed and lips parted as he examines me. I would have never imagined how similar his thinking expression is to the hazy, pleasure of when his cock fucks my fist; now I'll think of it every time I see him deep in thought. "I've never been with a trans guy before. I want to do it right."

"Like this." I adjust his fingers, showing him how to touch me, how to move his hand to stroke me perfectly. His dark eyes analyze every microexpression as he experiments, until he nods in satisfaction and kisses me. His mouth is blazing hot against my lips, my jaw, my neck, my collarbone, the bristle of his mustache a delicious rasp against my sensitive skin.

"Can I blow you, too?" he murmurs against my chest. I can only moan my reply, helpless and desperate as I gasp under his ministrations. His hand strokes me through my boxers so firmly, so perfectly, I might come before he gets a chance to.

I can feel his smirk against my skin, the puff of air from his chuckle on my nipple. "Or would you prefer I keep doing this?"

I babble helplessly, barely managing to form a "please," though I don't know which option I'm begging for.

I hate when his hand leaves me to pull at the waistband of my boxers, but I eagerly lift my hips so he can slide them down my legs. The delayed gratification is worth every painful second when his mouth trails hot down my stomach, my hips, finally pausing at my dick.

"What do you like?" Sanzhar asks, his breath lighting up every nerve ending, and it takes every ounce of self-control I have to keep my hips still. "Or anything you don't like?"

"Honestly, pretty much the same as most guys: don't use teeth," I chuckle, then add in a hurry, "Oh, but no gagging, please!"

His brow furrows as Sanzhar pulls the blanket so close around him, that all I can see is his endearing thinking face between my thighs. "Why would I gag?"

"One guy did that, because he thought it'd be affirming, as if my dick was big enough to choke on." I shrug. "But the boy smell was new, I was insecure about it, and I'm not proud of this, but I did cry. Absolutely killed the mood."

"But you smell incredible." With a deep, slow inhale, Sanzhar kisses the crease of my thigh, his brown eyes so earnest that I can't help but smile. "I will do my best to make this experience affirming for you, and not make you cry, and—"

"Tursyn, just suck me off already," I interrupt with a grin, my cheeks hot. This nerd is going to ruin me.

He levels that cute, annoyed look at me, but finally puts his mouth on me. Tentative at first (because that's who Sanzhar is), he gives me a few experimental licks. Glasses crooked, he watches my reaction, the way I bite my lip, or my sharp intake of breath with each swirl of his hot tongue around the engorged head. With a minuscule, satisfied nod, the same as every time he solves a problem, Sanzhar sucks me hard.

Within seconds, I am a trembling, begging mess for him. For someone who has never gone down on a trans guy before, Sanzhar is a quick study. With each slippery pull of his lips down my hypersensitive dick, his head bobs in a way that makes my chest burst with euphoria. Pleasure climbs higher and higher. Far too soon, I'm arching my back, lightheaded from the orgasm shaking my body.

As I lay on my back, panting and pushing Sanzhar's relentless mouth away from me, my head spins. The afterglow has lights streaking across my blurry vision. A fleeting glimmer in the dark, a gleam of green against the stars.

That isn't the stars from my orgasm; the glimmer is joined by another, and another.

"S—Sanzhar," I gasp, excitement coursing through me. I grasp for whatever parts of him I can reach, his shoulder, his forearm.

Sanzhar merely hums, kissing the soft skin of my thighs, nuzzling me with a tentative lick to my dick. "Can I keep going?"

"No, Sanzhar, look!" A laugh bursts out of me as I gesture skyward. Ribbons of green and blue ripple across the black, illuminating the spruce trees surrounding our dome. My hands tighten, fingertips digging into the meat of his arms.

He looks up, eyebrows raised. "Oh! Cool! Can I keep going?"

"Really? Cool? That's it?" With a laugh, I sit up to kiss his forehead. "We both flew to Alaska and lost our fucking jobs just for this! We got mulled wine waiting to split while we watch them, ate dinner early—this whole elaborate plan that you came up with, on the off chance we might see the aurora tonight. Here they are, and *you* would rather go down on me?"

"I'm not done yet," Sanzhar says simply, then smirks. "Based on how quickly you came the first time, I won't miss too much of the show."

Delight courses through me like adrenaline, and I can't help but laugh when I kiss him, loving the musky taste of myself on his lips, the mess I've made of his mustache.

"Rory, pour yourself some wine, sit back and enjoy. I'll join you when I'm done." Sanzhar nods to the thermos and mugs waiting for us next to our phones. "I was just getting good at it."

I reach over, and pour the still-steaming mulled wine. Because Sanzhar is right; his wine won't have a chance to cool off, unless he plans on edging me.

"Do you like penetration at all?" he asks, squeezing my thighs as if he can't wait to bury his face between them again.

"I like it when it's gentle, and there's a lot of lube involved." I screw the lid back on the thermos to keep the rest of the wine warm. "And only a finger or two."

"And...do you have lube, by any chance?" Sanzhar prompts, the eager gleam in his eyes highlighted by the swirls of green around us. His hair is rumpled, glasses smudged and crooked, and I can't help but smile. He's a completely different Sanzhar from the quiet, unassuming man I used to know.

Conveniently, my bathroom bag is still on the nightstand from our argument earlier. From my quart-sized bag, I fish the travel bottle of lube and toss it to him. "Yes sir, lube was one of my liquids. Don't judge."

"Can't judge when I'm the one who wants it." Sanzhar's body wiggles in excitement under the blanket as he uncaps it. He waits until I've settled against the pillows and headboard, lets me have a few sips of my wine, before he silently begs me with that irresistible pout of his.

With a chuckle, I give him a nod, and he eagerly settles between my thighs again, squirting lube onto his fingers.

It's almost sweet, how he tucks the blanket in around my hips, but I know he's just doing it to keep himself warm. The blankets don't last long as it is; my legs tense, tightening around his shoulders the second he slips a finger inside me.

Sanzhar is gentle. Slow strokes ease into a steady pace, his brown eyes examining me as he devours my dick. With a contented sigh, I lean back against the pillow, the urgency from my first orgasm gone. Maybe he does intend to edge me, because the rough eagerness from earlier is absent. Though this slow, unhurried pleasure is just as thrilling.

A surreal sense of disbelief settles over me as I sip my wine, the sweet spices warming me from the inside. I'm naked in a geodesic dome in the middle of Alaska, staring up at the inky sky alight with dancing ribbons of green and blue, the occasional streak of pink brightening the stars. A sight I've always longed to see, though I never imagined it'd be quite so beautiful. Nor did I imagine that I'd be getting sucked off by Sanzhar while I watch them. A mere three days ago, he was one of my least favorite people in the world, and now his mouth is occupied with pleasuring me simply because he wants to.

My breath catches at how unbelievably stunning he is like this. Lips shiny and swollen, eyes wide and piercing in the dim light. I stroke his hair and tell him how beautiful he is, how good he is at sucking me off, how to touch me—there, just like that, perfect—and how amazing he's making me feel.

My back arches when I come again, eyes watering and a sob escaping from the force of my orgasm. The aurora above seems to shimmer. The last drops of warm wine spill down my neck and chest as my body seizes with pleasure, trembling uncontrollably.

Fingers slipping out of me, Sanzhar kisses his way up my body, licking the line of wine off my chest and nibbling at my neck.

"Get your ass over here!" I pull him closer, loving the taste of me on his tongue, the smell of me soaked into his mustache, the self-satisfied hum of laughter at my eagerness. With a nudge of his shoulders, I push him to lay back against my chest, cradling him between my legs. "You had your fun, now enjoy the fucking aurora while I have mine."

"Oh?" Sanzhar chuckles as he lays his head against my shoulder. "Oh, this is stunning. Rory, look at how gorgeous that is!"

"You done missed most of it!" I laugh, passing him his mug, leaving my empty one on the table. "You don't have to be so generous, you know."

"Priorities." Sanzhar shrugs, sipping the wine. It makes me wonder what vulnerability he might be hiding in that nonchalance.

I kiss his neck. "Can I use a vibe on you when I jerk you off?"

"Oh!" He chuckles, staring up at the sky. "Is that your idea of fun?"

"As long as you want that, yes sir, it is." Slipping my hand under his arm, I caressing his stomach and hip, teasing where I want to go if he lets me.

"I won't say no," Sanzhar settles into my arms with that cute, quiet huff he always makes. "But don't take it personally if I fall asleep right after. Getting myself off is an essential part of my bedtime routine, and now my body is conditioned to knock out after. Probably why I've had trouble sleeping on this trip. There's no good place to jerk off when you're sharing a dome with your coworker."

"Trust me, I know the feeling." Smiling against his neck, I reach for my bathroom bag again for the bullet vibe that has gone unused this whole trip. I'm jealous of how hard Sanzhar must sleep normally if *this* has been poor. I feel around the bed for the bottle of lube, finally finding it wedged under his luscious ass, to coat my hand before wrapping it around his cock, stroking him to full hardness, his skin soft, hot, slick against my palm and fingers.

Sanzhar curses under his breath, biting his lip as I form a tight ring with my fingers and drag it over the flared head of his cock. Keeping my eyes on him—because I love learning what people like, analyzing how they react, memorizing each microexpression—I admire how the dancing lights brighten his glowing skin. When I press my thumb just right, he squeezes his eyes shut with a choked moan.

"Keep them open, enjoy the view," I nip his earlobe. Once he does, I reward him. Clicking the bullet onto the lowest setting, I drag it down his shaft, circle his balls, drawing a whimper from him. It turns into a strangled groan when I press it hard into his perineum. He becomes a wiggling mess in my arms. His hips buck so hard, I'm worried he might spill his wine, so I pin his legs down with my thighs. It's thrilling, to have him at my mercy like this, to have him gasping and begging and writhing in my arms.

"I hate you," Sanzhar whines when I take the bullet away. His broad chest heaves, shiny with sweat in the glimmering lights above.

"Funny way of showing it," I tease, swiping my thumb over his leaking slit. I nuzzle his neck. "You could tell me to stop."

"Don't you dare!" Sanzhar huffs. I let him catch his breath and take a swallow of wine, before I start stroking again, teasing him with the vibe. I don't plan on stopping again until I discover what that expressive, charming face does when he comes.

I don't have to wait long. Pressing the vibe against his perineum in time with my long, slow strokes, my fingers tightening around the head to draw a quiet grunt from him every time, turns one of those soft chuffs into a loud curse.

I flinch in surprise when something hot lands on my chin and the base of my throat.

Sanzhar mutters an "oh no," and I laugh at the source of his distress: cum covers his neck and chest, and his hand with the mug.

"Don't laugh!" Sanzhar groans, laughing himself. "I got cum in my wine!"

"And your hair!" My grin hurts as I click the vibe off to wipe the strand of hair stuck to his neck. His decolletage is shiny in the dark from the mess he's made of himself. I wish it were brighter, to see how flushed his cheeks are, how dilated his pupils have become. I groan just imagining it. "Stars, you're so fucking hot like this."

"I've never used a toy before," Sanzhar admits, finding his undershirt among the sheets to wipe my chin off. He smiles sheepishly as he cleans his hand. "Caught me off guard, Callahan."

"Good." I kiss his cheek, delighted that I've brought him a fraction of the pleasure he brought me. "I know you probably want to nap, or clean up, but it looks like this is fading," I gesture up at the northern lights with the vibe. Already the streaks of pink are absent, the bright blues losing ground to the quiet greens that started the display. "Should we wait until it ends?"

"Can you hand me my phone?" Sanzhar asks. "Better yet, can you take a picture? My hands are sticky, but I want to send something to my mom."

With the only hand between us not covered in lube and cum, I grab his phone to take a few photos. On the screen, the aurora appears brighter and bolder than what we can see. With Sanzhar's permission, I take one barely visible selfie of us, our shapes mere outlines in the darkness.

We haven't taken a single photo together yet on this trip. But if this works out, this is a memory of us I want to capture.

A feeling I want to come back to: tipsy—from our mutual pleasure more than the wine we've had—and awe-filled at the beauty surrounding us, the companionship we've found in each other. If this is our first adventure we're experiencing together, I never want to forget it.

Tuesday

Chapter Fifteen

The dome looks strange without all of our stuff scattered everywhere. The late morning dawn finally breaks, revealing our absence before we've even left. There wasn't much space to take up, considering half of the dome is the enormous bed. But with my duffel stuffed full, and Sanzhar's hard-sided rolling bag waiting by the trapdoor, the room feels empty.

"Do we have to go back?" I ask, hugging Sanzhar from behind as he wedges his liquids into a clear zippered pouch. His hair and skincare routine is much more involved than mine—his bag is bursting at the seams, and there are more bottles scattered on the bed. "Do you want to put any of that in my bag?"

"Oh my god, yes please! I don't know how I got all of this here in the first place." Sanzhar plants a kiss on my cheek. "And yes, we have to go back. I don't really want to either, but we have to rescue your Blahaj and return our laptops before Bill gets back from his trip."

I groan, but he has a point. It's better to rip the Band-Aid of our new reality off. "Gina texted me this morning. Bill asked her to draft up a termination notice for both of us. Best case scenario, I reckon, because we can both file for unemployment if the situation at your old company takes a while, or falls through completely." I snort. "Sorry, I'm not the most optimistic person when you get to know me. I just hide my cynical side at work."

"That's a relief, honestly," Sanzhar laughs. "You're far too patient and sweet with everyone. They don't deserve you."

"Me?" I tease, kissing his neck, pulling him tight against my chest. "You're so stoic and calm, Gina and I didn't think it was even worth starting a betting pool for when you'd crack and snap at Bill."

"Well, the good news is, everyone at my old job is genuinely great, now that the red flag is gone, so we don't need to fake anything anymore," Sanzhar huffs. "And Emmy says to have our resumes ready, and HR will open positions for us right after New Year's. There's also an admin retiring in May, for Gina, right when her leave should be ending."

"This is really happening, ain't it?" I ask quietly. That surreal feeling of "how did I get here?" is slowly starting to feel real. For once, I'm starting to trust that this warm glow in my sternum might stick around. "We never have to see Bill again."

"Oh, I love the sound of that." Sanzhar smiles as he leans back against me. "What are your plans for Friday?"

"Christmas, you mean?" I scoff. "Literally just another day these days, honestly. Why, what are you doing?"

"You, hopefully."

I choke on my own spit, a flush burning through my whole body. I shouldn't be surprised at this point, but every time Sanzhar says something remotely raunchy, I can't help but get flustered.

"Sorry, that sounded way more sexual than I intended!" Sanzhar giggles, but I don't buy the innocence in his tone; he knew exactly what that would do to me. "I was suggesting you join my annual Lord of the Rings marathon. Maybe stay the night, or the whole weekend, depending on how long it takes us to watch it?"

"You said you watch the extended version, right?" I ask, pretending to ponder the idea, as if the answer is going to be anything but a huge, resounding yes.

Sanzhar tsks, "Of course."

"Can I bring cinnamon rolls?" My heart twinges at the memory of my family's traditions. Even if I'll likely never spend Christmas morning with them again, at least I can bring some of my nostalgia to Sanzhar's traditions.

"You *bake*?!" Sanzhar hums, turning around to drape himself over me and plant a kiss on my cheek. I love how affectionate he is, how right he feels in my arms. "I had no idea you were so talented, Callahan."

"You just want garlic bread, don't you?" I tease. I learned to bake to impress Sarah back when we first met; I will have to thank her sweet tooth for helping me impress Sanzhar, too.

"I'm not dignifying that with a response," Sanzhar laughs, turning back to finish packing.

With a smile that won't fade, I busy myself with turning down the airflow on the woodstove, tidying up the mess we've left behind in three days, gathering up all signs of December Rory and Sanzhar Sprint One existing here.

Even if I still can't quite believe how the stars have aligned so perfectly in a mere weekend, what we've found together is a miracle I do not take for granted. Sanzhar is someone so resilient, as considerate and lonely as I've been. I thought we were rivals when we could have been allies, strangers when we could have been friends, alone when we could have been companions. But now we are all of that, and more.

Reality may change the magic we found together, but December Rory and Sanzhar Sprint Two is about to begin, and I can't wait to see what we create together.

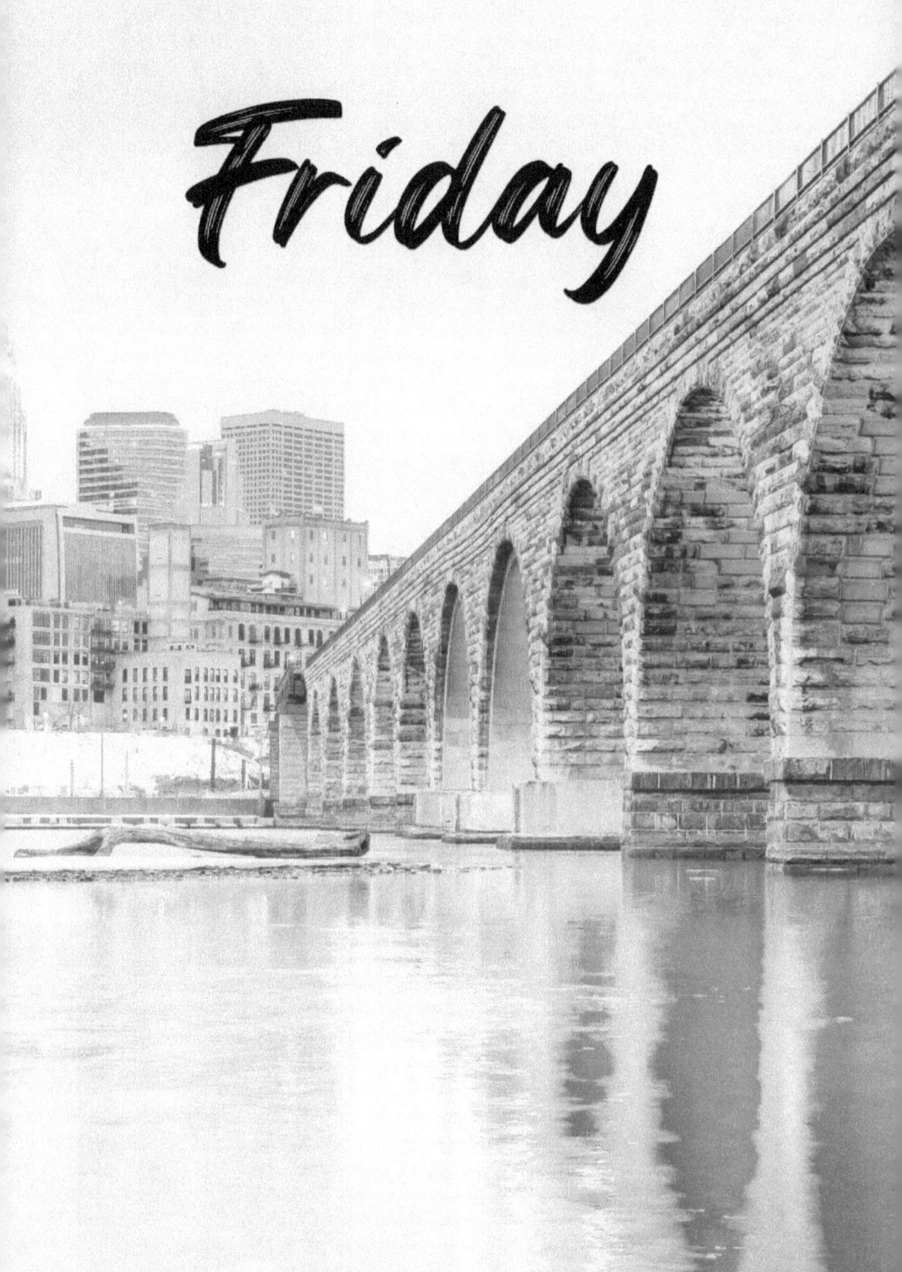
Friday

EPILOGUE

"DO WE HAVE TO say it?" I ask, grinning because I already know the answer.

"You know we do," Sanzhar smiles as he lays on my bare chest. His glasses shine blue from the glow of the TV in the dark room. "It's basically a law."

We both wait for the angry shout from the surround sound to die down, before we say, "Did you know Viggo broke his toe when he kicked the helmet?" then burst into laughter. Sanzhar buries his giggles into the crux of my neck as he clings to me, making me delirious with happiness.

We're stretched out on his couch, enjoying the feel of each other's skin on ours as we cuddle, buried in one of the many blankets he's stashed around his otherwise-tidy apartment. Sanzhar's place is a quick light rail ride away, down the Blue Line in Longfellow, with the stop close enough we can hear the bells from the crossing gates whenever the train goes by. Convenient, and yet, I have no desire to leave this couch anytime soon.

From how he's wrapped around me, miles of our bare skin pressed together under the blanket, Sanzhar seems to feel the same. We fooled around a bit earlier, as the credits for the Fellowship scrolled, and didn't bother getting dressed again. But for the most part, our day together has been more affectionate than anything.

I love how we can't stop touching each other, even though we spent all day Wednesday and Thursday night together, too. I'm sure we'll find a balance once we're working again, and the honeymoon glow settles into something sustainable, with a little more alone time. But for right now, I'm loving every second of December Rory and Sanzhar Sprint Two.

Once our giggles die down, I build up my courage. I've been thinking about this since I rode the train here last night, a pan of homemade cinnamon rolls in hand, ready to be baked this morning. "What are you doing next Friday?"

"Probably nothing." Sanzhar shrugs, and my chest tightens; Sanzhar's too chalant to shrug over nothing. I narrow my eyes, wondering if I should press him. But he asks the follow up, "Why?" before I can.

"My polycule has an annual New Year's Eve party. Would you like to come?" I hold my breath, unreasonably nervous for something so simple. I don't even care if he doesn't want to—No, I do care a lot, but I would *understand* if he doesn't want to. This invitation feels rushed. A week ago, I loathed Sanzhar Tursyn and everything he stood for; now I'm inviting him to meet my chosen family. "It's casual, chill. Potluck and BYOB, with just a dozen or so of our close friends."

Sanzhar's lips part against my skin, and I know without looking that he has his deep-thinking face on. "As your friend, or coworker, or something more?"

"I'll be honest, I spent about three hours on the phone with Ducky yesterday gushing about you. Everybody's been roasting me something fierce in the group chat since." I rub my face, cheeks burning as Sanzhar looks up at me. I peek through my fingers to make sure he's smiling. To my relief, he's downright smug. "But I don't want you to feel like it's a 'meet the family' situation, even though it kind of is. More like a 'welcome to my social circle, where you will happen to meet my chosen family' kind of deal."

It's well past my niece's bedtime, and not one single person in my birth family has even sent me a text. But the hollow ache in my chest hurts less with Sanzhar's thick body and comforting presence grounding me. As much as I miss the past, I want to be where I'm wanted, supported, appreciated. And right now, that's right here, with Sanzhar.

"But that don't mean it's necessarily romantic!" I add in a rush, as the silence makes me question if this might be too much, too soon for Sanzhar's aversion to committed relationships. "It can be however you want, platonic, or queerplatonic, or otherwise. If you want to come as my friend, I can tell my other partners to stuff it with any teasing or interrogations. I know this is new, but my polycule is important to me, and I can tell you're going to be important, too. You already are! And I would like for you to meet them. I think you'd get along with them, and—"

"Callahan," Sanzhar presses his fingers to my lips, "My delayed response wasn't a no, I was just simply thinking it through. I will come to your New Year's party, as someone whose exact relationship to you is as of yet undefined. Because you're important to me, too, and I would like to meet your other partners. I have one request, though— Well, two." He chuckles against my chest.

"What's that now?" I murmur, stroking his hair away from his face. I'll give Sanzhar anything he wants.

"If no one else has claimed it yet, I would like to kiss you at midnight." His face flushes. "It feels so cheesy to admit this, but

I've always wanted to do that, like they do in the movies, and I've never had a person to share that with at New Year's before."

"Done. Anytime, anywhere you want a kiss, I'm down." I curl up to kiss his forehead now. "What's the second thing?"

Sanzhar grins, that crooked smile a light that makes my heart pound. "Any chance you're bringing garlic bread to this potluck?"

A laugh escapes me, and Sanzhar devolves into giggles along with me. I would have understood if he didn't want to come, wasn't ready to be a part of the rest of my life. But my body is flooded with relief and exhilaration that he wants to, only asking for a mere kiss and a snack. A token compared to how much joy, hope, and inspiration he's brought me over the past week. "For you? Anything."

Acknowledgements

Thank you to myself, first and foremost, because wow! Writing and publishing a novella so much less work than a massive four-book series! Let's do more of these!

In all seriousness, I want to thank my editor Mikko Lahna at Quick Fox Editors for their support with this lovely, fun, and self-indulgent project. I made Rory extra-dense, just for you, to amp up the Idiots-to-Lovers. Because if I'm writing a trans and ace-inclusive secular holiday novella purely for my own self interest, you should enjoy it too!

I also want to thank Otte, who designed the cover for me. I went into this with some very specific requirements and very little understanding of design, and I think you nailed it out of the fucking park! It's exactly what I had in mind, and more!

Thank you to Kirsten, Sam, Precy, Nik, and Dan for authenticity/beta reading this for me. You helped these characters come alive and shape their stories!

In the course of writing this, two major storm systems struck western Alaska in rapid succession, causing extensive damage to local communities. If you are in a financial position to do so, please consider donating to the Alaska Community Foundation at https://alaskacf.org/ and consider yourself part of these acknowledgements as well. I will be donating 25% of the profits from *Glimmer in the Dark* to this foundation, so any reviews and recommendations of this book will aid long-term disaster relief efforts in the area. Thank you, readers, for your support!

Also by Cozy

If you enjoyed this book (or if you didn't!), please kindly show your support by leaving a review and telling your friends about it. Honest reviews and word-of-mouth recommendations make it possible for indie authors to keep writing. Thank you!

Want to read more by Cozy? Check out their books at cozydubois.com

***Confession* Series**

Book 1: *Loving Lee*

Book 2: *Love on the Sunny Side*

Book 3: *Tempting Tara*

Book 4: *Carte Blanche*

Epilogue: *Finally Phineas* coming soon!

Standalone Novels

Earthly Ties

Summer Weddings in Solberg
Petty Roots
Familiar Faces

Long Nights and Bright Futures
Glimmer in the Dark
Dancing in the Snow coming November 2026

Sleighbell Springs
For Luck's Sake
Happy (Endings) for the Holidays coming December 2026
Searching for Starlight coming November 2027
More Happy (Endings) for the Holidays coming December 2027

Short Stories
"Dad, Are You..." — part of *Bi All Accounts: Volume 1.*

About the Author

Cozy DuBois (they/them) thought writing fiction was a long-lost hobby. A longtime lover of romance novels, Cozy has renewed their love for writing by telling stories for and about LGBTQ+ people. They hope to bring more books into the world that represent the complex and entangled relationships between friends, lovers, and chosen family found in the queer community they love.

Based in Minneapolis, they enjoy life with their partner, two hound dogs, a regal queen of a cat, dozens of houseplants, and a garden that has seen better days. Find them with a beverage in hand on a patio anytime the temp is above freezing or planning their next vacation when it's not.

Connect with Cozy on social media or via email updates at cozydubois.com for announcements about upcoming releases.

www.ingramcontent.com/pod-product-compliance
Lightning Source LLC
Chambersburg PA
CBHW060033060826
49398CB00032B/382

* 9 7 8 1 9 6 4 3 8 6 0 9 6 *